Retribution Trail

Eb Bream didn't think life could get any worse. His wife had run off with another man, making him the joke of the town, he'd started hitting the bottle and had finally ended up cleaning spittoons in Jake's Saloon. But then Travis Kentish, son of a big shot rancher, made the mistake of trying to push Eb a step too far.

Now, on the run from a vengeful father, Eb is unaware of the dangers that lie ahead. A great many men will die as they ride the retribution trail and Eb is destined to face his greatest challenge.

Retribution Trail

M. DUGGAN

A Black Horse Western

ROBERT HALE · LONDON

ISBN-10: 0-7090-8014-X
ISBN-13: 978-0-7090-8014-5

Robert Hale Limited
Clerkenwell House
Clerkenwell Green
London EC1R 0HT

The right of M. Duggan to be identified as
author of this work has been asserted by her
in accordance with the Copyright, Designs and
Patents Act 1988.

Typeset by
Derek Doyle & Associates, Shaw Heath.
Printed and bound in Great Britain by
Antony Rowe Limited, Wiltshire.

CHAPTER ONE

Men whom he had regarded as friends were sniggering at him. And not behind his back. Disparaging remarks were made to the effect that he was a coward. He could not understand it, for what had happened was no one's concern but his own.

'I am a peaceable man,' was all he would say. 'And I aim to stay that way. I don't hold with killing unless a man is fighting for his life. I ain't in that position. Now leave me be to get on with my work.'

He was a telegraph clerk and as such was at the beck and call of the town. 'The way things are suits me just fine,' he said more than once. No one seemed to believe him, but it was true. He kinda not liked having his nagging wife Gracie around. But when he thought how she'd run off with a travelling salesman he found himself growing furiously angry. Murderous thoughts filled his head. But being of outstanding character he resolved not to act upon these thoughts. They must be buried deep. After all, he had first-hand experience of what a man who gave way to rage could do. Not that this murderously inclined rage had ever been directed towards himself and his grandma. In Grandma's house everyone said please and thank you. No one raised their voice and that included Grandpa. But outside the home the old man had become another person entirely.

'You stomp on them before they stomp on you,' was the creed Grandpa had lived by. 'You've got it in you, Eb. One day a luckless varmint is gonna find the key. I may not be around to see it but it's gonna happen.'

Well, the travelling salesman had turned the key but Eb had relocked the door, so to speak. But it was not funny. It was not a joke and they were all laughing.

'Just let me be,' he said but nobody seemed to hear him.

With Gracie gone he felt as though an ever-increasing burden had fallen from his shoulders. Even keeping his job did not seem important nowadays. When he was not at work sometimes he'd head for the cemetery just outside of town and sit himself down beside the graves of his ma and pa whom he could not remember, and his grandparents, whom he had loved dearly.

He closed the office for lunch now, something he had not done whilst his wife had been around. He was sitting back, resting against a headstone when his reflections were disturbed by a voice yelling out his name with an urgency which could not be denied.

He opened his eyes and scrambled to his feet, his first thought being that something had happened to Gracie. Heading his way was a small hunched figure hobbling along with the aid of a walking-cane. He frowned. It was unlikely old Annie would have come to find him to bring news of Gracie. The old lady seldom left her shack on the outskirts of town. He himself was scarcely acquainted with her. He could not imagine what she might want with him.

'Well here I am,' he rejoined. He hesitated. 'What's bothering you!'

Reaching him, she sat down. He found himself wondering whether she would need a hand up.

'I'm counting on you,' she quavered, 'Eb Bream, you are my only hope.'

'Well, if your shack needs patching up, naturally I'll see to it,' he heard himself say.

'Goddamn it, Eb Bream, I ain't here about my shack. I ain't got long left and it can fall down around my ears for all I care,' she replied cantankerously.

'Well then, ma'am, what is it you want?' He wiped his brow, which was perspiring.

'I want you to save my granddaughter,' she replied, not beating about the bush.

'Young Jacqueline?' He wondered if the girl were lost.

'Otto has got her locked in his cellar. He ain't gonna let her out. He's gonna leave her to starve to death, to die of thirst and there ain't no one in this two-bit town got the stomach to try and help her. But that is to be expected as Otto is such a mean son of a bitch.'

Very slowly Eb sat down beside her. 'Now, are you certain of your facts, ma'am.'

'Of course I am certain,' she snapped.

'And why has he locked her in the cellar?'

'Fact is Jacqueline is with child.' The old woman paused. 'Otto says she has brought shame upon the family. My Lucy is terrified of him. He knocks her around something bad if she dares say a word he thinks out of place or if his victuals don't suit.'

'Could it be he just aims to scare the girl? Could it be he aims to let her out pretty damn soon?' Eb enquired. There was a sinking feeling in the pit of his stomach. 'Now you think carefully before you answer me,' he advised.

She nodded. '1 am mortally sorry, Eb, but I am certain,' she replied.

'And what has Lucy done about this.'

'First thing she did was approach Gordon the mayor. He's got the power to rustle up the men and confront Otto. He can swear them in as law officers when they are needed.'

'Gordon, huh!' Eb had sat next to Gordon at school.

'Well, Gordon claimed Lucy was deranged and making it all up. And Doc who was with Gordon, said that unless Lucy shut up he would be happy to certify her if Otto wanted her shipped to an asylum. Otto might even try to do it, for he does not care for Lucy on account of her having only girls. He says she has been cursed.'

'So no one in town will help,' Eb essayed slowly.

'No.'

'But you've heard the talk. Folk are calling me a coward on account of me not going after my

8

runaway wife and her new man!'

'Ah, but folk don't know you like your grandpa knew you. He thought highly of you, Eb. And he thought highly of your grandma, for all she believed in turning the other cheek. He always said you were his boy through and through.' She paused. 'I know what Kingdom would have done had he still been alive.'

Eb nodded. 'Probably Kingdom would scarcely be able to walk but I reckon his fury would be unabated. But the fact is he ain't here and I am.' Slowly he stood up. 'Do you want a hand up?'

'Why, thank you kindly, Eb, but you can't haul me up by the arm. You must lift me up carefully.'

Eb lifted her up.

'Well, Otto will soon figure out you're behind it if I show my nose. And that puts you in mortal danger. Maybe you ain't got long to go but I can't see you gone before your natural time has arrived. Nor can Otto be trusted to restrain himself in future. You get my drift?'

'I do, Eb. And I understand it goes against your natural inclinations, but the fact is there ain't no one else. Why, if I were twenty years younger I would tackle him myself, but jest getting out to find you has turned my legs to jelly. I can scarce walk. What it is to grow old. You young 'uns can't begin to under-stand.'

Eb glanced down at his grandpa's gravestone. He could almost hear the old man telling him to get on with it. And he guessed that was what he had to do. He touched the tip of his hat. 'Rest assured, ma'am, your granddaughter ain't going to die in her pa's cellar.'

'Thank you Eb. I'll be praying for you.'

Eb left her there. He made his way back to his own modest home and buckled on his gun belt. He holstered the Peacemaker with reluctance.

'Where the hell have you been?' As luck would have it Gordon was waiting to dispatch a telegram.

'I've been speaking to Annie,' Eb replied tersely. 'I understand you know what is going on.'

'A wise man does not concern himself with another man's family business,' Gordon rebuked. 'And if the girl sickens and dies, why, Otto may find himself better off with her out of the way. Indeed he suspects the girl was a mite too friendly with one of those redskins recently shipped to the reservation.' Gordon shook his head. 'Best let things be, Eb. You're good at that, ain't you?'

'I can't let things be,' Eb rejoined, 'for I am not that kind of man.'

'There ain't no one in this town, Eb, who will save you from Otto's justified wrath,' Gordon warned. He smirked. 'Your grandpa has been dead for many years, Eb. He cannot help you. You cannot expect to cash in on the Bream reputation, for we all know you are not the man he was.'

'Well, I never claimed to be,' Eb rejoined mildly. 'Indeed, my grandfather was unique but I know for sure he would never have locked a helpless girl in a cellar and left her to die of thirst and hunger. He never picked on the helpless. Nor did he allow himself to be swayed by the beliefs of others. His view was that none of us had the right to throw stones as we all had something to hide. And sure as hell Otto ain't got the right to starve his girl to death. Now if you'll step out of my way, Gordon, I must attend to this matter.'

'You go anywhere near Otto and you are fired.'

Eb shrugged. 'We'll see.'

'The town will follow my lead. Hell you may well be more dead than alive when Otto has finished with you. You'll be a liability.'

Eb didn't trouble himself listening to Gordon, who was soon busy telling other folk what was afoot. And folk being what they were, they seemed more than happy to troop along behind him. A few took it upon themselves to yell out that he ought to let things be. And others yelled that if he wanted to prove himself a man he ought set off after Gracie.

Otto made saddles. Damn good ones. And when Eb confronted him he was not alone: two of his cronies were lounging and passing the time of day as Otto worked. Eb came straight to the point:

'I know what you are about, Otto, and you must let your girl up out of the cellar.'

'You get the hell out of here. You meddling varmint,' warned Otto, his accent heavily accented. 'I ain't having no one tell me what to do. You're just a no-account telegraph clerk. From what I hear your grandpa was the big man, not you.'

'Well, I ain't interested in being a big man. My concern is to do what's right.'

'I'm gonna beat you to pulp.' Otto took a step forward.

Eb held up his hand. 'Are you threatening to kill me, Otto?'

'I'm gonna enjoy this. She ain't seeing daylight again.'

'Let's make the bastard dance and then we'll fill him full of holes,' Joe Coulter yelled. He reached for his gun.

Eb found himself reacting instinctively. He reached for his Peacemaker and blasted Joe Coulter, aiming for his heart. That way there would be no chance of Coulter's firing a second shot. Otto meanwhile, was heading towards him, eyes bulging and face contorted with fury. Eb shot him as well, knowing he would have no chance if Otto were to grab him for Otto was built like a bull and Gracie had often compared Eb to a beanpole, he being so thin and all. Vince Gatrell was luckier, for Eb shot him through the shoulder and stomped on his gun hand for good measure. Not that Gatrell was by any means a gunfighter; Gatrell was by profession a farmer and slow when it came to hauling iron.

An object hard and heavy struck Eb on the shoulder. He whirled, gun ready. Gatrell's boy, aged about twelve, had hefted a rock and for a moment was almost a gonner as Eb's mind tried to connect with his trigger finger. The bullet struck the dirt to the left of the boy's foot. The boy fled with a howl.

Shocked faces regarded Eb.

'Anyone else got anything to say,' he yelled. 'No! Good. Then I aim to get the girl out of the cellar.

And then I aim to leave this no-account town. But I'll be back. Jest to make sure all is well. And if anyone of you varmints has done wrong, Lord help me, we all know what Kingdom was capable of and I guess I am too.'

'You had no call to kill him. You had no call to kill my man,' Lucy whined as Eb opened the trap-door leading down to the cellar. But he reckoned she was just putting on a show for the benefit of anyone listening and she had already dispatched one of the other girls to bring water.

'Get the hell out of here and leave us be!' Lucy yelled, speaking not to Eb but to interested observers. 'All you varmints who were happy to see my girl die!' As she was speaking she was hauling Jacqueline from the cellar. 'And in case anyone is interested, Joe Coulter was the father of this baby. He paid Otto for the privilege and now he has got his just deserts.'

'Even so, Eb, you have overstepped the mark. You're still fired,' Gordon observed sanctimoniously.

Eb thinned his lips. 'Well then, Gordon, I reckon I'm entitled to do something to justify my sacking.' So saying he punched Gordon hard in the mouth. It was time Gordon got his deserts!

His world had collapsed. His wife had left him for a travelling salesman, no less. And folks in this town were now turned against him, unable to see that he had righted a great wrong. He'd killed two men and badly injured another and had almost blasted a young boy for good measure.

Hell, he needed a drink.

CHAPTER TWO

'I need a man!' The woman's voice was too loud. The sound of it made Bream's head ache even more. Whoever she was she was standing at the entrance to the alleyway running alongside the general store. He was at the end of the alleyway, tucked away out of sight behind piled refuse where he had collapsed last night unable even to make his way to the livery stable and his horse. Lord, he could not even pay the stableman. He needed money real bad!

Goddamn it! The sound of her voice was enough to drive a man crazy. All he wanted was for her to hoof it, fool that she was, discussing her private concerns out on Main Street where anyone could hear. He didn't move. He wasn't interested enough to raise his head or even bat an eyelid. And should she glance down the alleyway all she would see would be a pair of worn old boots sticking out from behind a trash barrel.

'A stupid man!' she continued.

Well, that sure is me, he thought. Why had he not seen what everyone else had? His wife Gracie had thought him a goddamn bore.

'A man whose luck is due to run out.'

His luck had run out. His wife was gone and his goddamn pockets were empty. And he had lost his job. Not that he would ever go back to it!

'And above all he must be a fast and accurate shooter!'

'Well, that's me,' he muttered. Maybe if he had blasted a few *hombres* whilst she was around Gracie would have thought more highly of him.

'You're just day-dreaming, Maud. There ain't no way you're gonna find a man fool enough to challenge Floyd Peters. A top gun like maybe Pilgrim would do it but you ain't got that kind of cash available. If you want Floyd dead – and you have every reason to – why, I reckon you will have to find a way of achieving that end yourself. But have a care! They hang women for murder!'

'I'll think of something but I guess in the meanwhile I must string him along. There ain't no way that varmint is going to get his hands on my ranch.' She snorted with disgust. 'Nor on me! I'm telling you, Howie, I'm a woman riled!'

'I reckon you are Maud, I reckon you are,' the oldster agreed. Bream could tell the speaker was an oldster from his querulous tone. Their voices were fading now as they moved away.

Bream propped himself up against the wall. He was tempted to root among the garbage to see if there was anything to eat. His stomach growled. His head pounded. But he was not in the least tempted to apply for the job of gunning down the *hombre*

Floyd. Killing for money, well, he'd always thought that was as low as a man could get. He had not sunk that low yet. True his wife had run off with a salesman and Gracie had also helped herself to their savings. And if that was not bad enough the whole town had bad-mouthed him because he had not set off in pursuit of the pair.

Significantly no one had insulted him after he had killed Otto. Folk had scurried out of his path as though he was a mad dog. Faces that had once smiled at him in happier days had regarded him with fear. And he had not liked this. He did not wish to be known as a fast and dangerous gun. But he had killed and there was no going back to being good old Eb Bream, telegraph clerk.

He had not gone after the varmints because he could not trust himself not to blast the pair of them. Retribution was a dangerous thing. It led men down paths they ought not to take. He was not going to let the pair turn him into a no-account killer, so he'd dug in his heels and flatly refused to go after them even though the whole goddamn town of Shorts told him he had right on his side. He was better than that. He did not need to kill to prove his worth.

By his side lay the whiskey-bottle he had emptied last night during his search for oblivion. Well, there wasn't any way he was going to ride out of this town today. He was in no condition to sit a horse even if he could get it out of the livery.

He closed his eyes. He must stay put until he was steady on his feet. A drunk was a sitting target for those with a mean streak. And there were plenty of such men about. They did it because they knew that they could. The gun and the boot ruled! Being decent would not save a man from being blasted. Town bums were considered a lawful target. And, Lord help him, he was on the way to becoming a town bum. It had to stop. He was never going to touch a drop of strong liquor again.

He stayed put until it was midday or thereabouts. He felt stiff and hunger gnawed his vitals. He stank of sweat and stale whiskey, but as he lurched to his feet he told himself that his life was gonna start over. This was the last time he would hit the bottle. Before Gracie had run off he had been content to be a telegraph clerk, even though he had initially wanted to be a railway man travelling the country along with the tracks, but she would have none of that! He guessed he would have remained a telegraph clerk until his fingers were too rheumaticky to hit the keys.

He lurched from the alleyway and, walking as tall as he was able, he made it to the horse-trough. He plunged his head into the water and gulped down mouthfuls. He was through feeling sorry for himself. Some men went under but not him!

'Get out of my way, bum! My horse wants to drink.'

He straightened up; a tall thin man, a harmless-enough-looking fellow, he knew, but even the worse for drink he could have dealt with the young man, if needs be! He moved away from the horse-trough, wondering if the rider was looking for trouble. But the man ignored him.

He was no bum! There was no way he was going to end up the town drunk. Every town seemed to have one, the butt of malicious jokes. Maybe he could earn himself a meal and pay for his horse's care by shovelling out the stalls.

HOWIE'S LIVERY the sign read. Last night it had been too dark for him to notice.

'Howie,' Bream guessed, was the same man who had been palavering with Miss Maud. And there was Howie himself, a weather-lined oldster, as tough as old leather and bowed by time but not apparently mellowed, for the cantankerous old devil's first move was to dispatch a gob of chewing tobacco towards the toe of Bream's old boot.

'Have you got any work?' Bream croaked. Another man might have felt inclined to blast the old fool. In fact Bream did feel inclined but as he was not toting a shooter Howie was safe.

'I don't hire bums,' Howie declared maliciously. 'Besides which I have all the help I need.' He indicated a strong-looking farm boy who had just appeared round a corner of the barn. 'Now get on your way,' he addressed Bream. 'What do you take me for! A damn fool! And you ain't getting your horse till you pay the bill. I've heard all the hard-luck stories there are to hear. And let me tell you I ain't moved by them. Now get!'

Bream resisted the urge to grab hold of that scrawny neck and shake the old fellow the way a dog would shake a rat. Without saying a word he turned and trudged wearily away. The world was full of the likes of Howie. He left the livery barn and headed back towards Main Street. There were two saloons that might be hiring. The first told him to get the hell out of it, the second, Jake's Place, offered work.

'I've lost the old bum I used to employ so I'll guess you'll do,' Jake advised with a leer.

Bream did not much care for Jake. Jake wore his long blond hair to his shoulders and wore a fringed buckskin jacket. 'You can swab the floor and clean out the spittoons,' the man sneered. 'Anything left in the bottom of the glasses you get to swig.'

'How much are you paying?' Bream asked. It was a pittance, just about enough to keep his horse stabled and buy a meal. Hell, if he were careful, why, he'd even be able to afford a soak at the bath-house and a hair-cut and shave from time to time.

'You can start as from now,' Jake grunted.

Bream nodded. Silently he set to work. He swabbed the goddamn floor and cleaned the spittoons. 'I want paying by the day,' he said. 'I need to eat.' For one moment he thought Jake was going to refuse to pay up, but Jake nodded, then spat into a nearby spittoon.

'Sure you do, you goddamn bum,' he observed with a shrug as he dropped a coin into the spittoons. Silently Bream retrieved his wages.

'I'm gonna eat,' he said, 'and then I'll be back to clean.' Without even glancing at Jake he quit the saloon. Goddamnit, he felt an urge to blast the saloonkeeper. Shaking his head, he headed for the town's sole eating-house. Could this be called being on the way up, he thought drily. Maybe or maybe not! His situation was precarious. Good-hearted Jake might, on a whim, decide to terminate his employment. Jake was clearly an *hombre* who didn't give a damn about anyone other than himself and would doubtless find pleasure in stringing him along for a week or two before firing him.

But then all Bream needed was a small stake to see him on to the next town. Sure as hell he did not aim to settle in this two-bit town. What the hell was it called? He looked around for a sign. Yep, there it was. WELCOME TO KENTISH he read. And the sign was freshly painted, which made a change. He reckoned this meant the Kentish family was big in these parts.

Tony Kentish saw himself as an important man who commanded respect. His Grandpa had founded the town. Men feared him. But his goddamn wife did not fear him and he hated the sight of her. She was screeching at him now.

'You've broken the rules. No boots in the house. You've tramped dirt into my parlour.' Emily's voice rose progressively. It ended in a screech.

'I'm sorry, my dear. But Travis is to blame. I'll have it cleaned up.' He took a deep breath and hollered for the Mexican maid, Juanita, who was almost as fat and ugly as his wife.

'My heart!' Emily pressed a hand to her heaving bosom. 'See what you have done!'

'You go lie down. I'll have Juanita bring you tea.' He was desperate. He knew what was on the way. She did not disappoint him. Emily began to rant and rave. She cried and screamed until she ran out of steam. Only then did she head for her bedroom. His hope was that she'd lie up for a week or so complaining of ill health while Juanita waited on her hand and foot. Goddamnit, how much better life would be without her!

And Travis, varmint that he was, had deliberately trampled mud over the prize carpet. This was his idea of a laugh!

'Travis!' From inside the house Juanita heard the boss bellowing for his son. That he put up with this behaviour from his son continued to surprise her, for he was a hard, unyielding man, a man who had hung a rustler from the old tree growing just in front of the ranch-house porch. Juanita had watched from the window while the rustler had slowly choked to death. She shook her head; the son Travis was worse than his father, for Travis would hurt others without reason. But perhaps today Travis had made a mistake. His father was real mad.

'You little varmint,' Tony yelled. 'You've gone and upset your ma!'

Travis smirked. And then he made a fatal error of judgement. 'So?' He aimed a gobbet of spit at his pa's boot.

Tony sucked in his breath. The men, leastways some of the crew, had witnessed the incident and he knew that if the men did not respect their boss, well hell, a man could not run his ranch. Travis had yet to recognize this fact. And it was about time he did. Tony drew back his hand and struck Travis hard across the face. Travis almost reached for his shooter. The only thing that stopped him was the fact that he was not quite sure he could outdraw the old man. His pa was fast. So he did the next best thing.

21

'To hell with you, Pa!' he yelled. 'I'm heading for town.'

Tony did not try to stop his headstrong son. He jerked his head towards two of his men, Shield and Bainbridge.

'Ride along with him. I want him back safe.' He glanced at the sky which was darkening, a sure sign a freak storm was brewing. Some goddamn bum was going to get the stuffing beaten out of him tonight. Travis was in a foul mood. Well, maybe he would calm down by the time he got back home. His pa, one time or another, would have whopped every man on the crew. There was no shame in it. Nor could a man be expected to raise his hand to his pa.

'You call me "sir",' Jake had ordered.

Bream had nodded. 'Yes, sir,' he'd heard himself say. He reckoned his grandpa was turning in his grave, for he had never believed in servility. His grandpa would have smashed Jake's face against the bar and thought nothing of it.

'There ain't much difference between us,' his grandpa had often observed, 'except that I run on a short fuse and you run on a long fuse. You'll see, boy, you'll see!'

Bream always shook his head. He did not want to see. All he wanted to do was keep his head down, earn a few dollars, save a few dollars and get himself a small stake, enough for him to move on to another town. He aimed to follow that fine example set by the tumbleweed. He would go where fancy took him. So he collected spittoons and washed them. He collected glasses and washed them. He swabbed the floor. But he never ever helped himself to the dregs remaining in the glasses. He ate once a day and his clothes were clean. He took a bath once a week and tried to save towards his stake. And that polecat Jake, seeing that he was not behaving the way a bum ought to behave, had taken to offering him whiskey on the house. Bream always thanked Jake kindly but replied that he felt obliged to refuse.

Now, as Bream collected glasses, Miz Jenny watched him with interest. She had taken to saying: 'You ain't always been a bum, Bream. How is it you're cleaning spittoons?'

'I ain't a proud man, Miz Jenny,' he always replied.

'There's more to you than meets the eye,' she would observe knowingly.

'I don't reckon so, Miz Jenny,' he always rejoined.

Now as Miz Jenny watched Bream at work it occurred to her that he might turn out to be a dangerous man if cornered. Bream reminded her of a kettle about to spout steam. He interested her. Few men did these days, but Eb Bream, with his quiet respectful manner, had caught her eye.

Jake was also watching Bream. He did not care for his new employee. Bream had shown himself to be a silent, taciturn man who made no effort to ingratiate himself with anyone. He did not smile. He did not play the buffoon. To his disbelief Jake had yet to see Bream touch a drop of liquor. Jake was puzzled. He would have booted Bream out save for the fact that sooner or later one of the patrons would decide to have some fun at the bum's expense. Patrons knew

Jake kept a shotgun behind the bar. They also knew he would not use it to save his pot man. Old Andy, Bream's predecessor, had been forced, under threat of having his toes blasted, to dance like a dancing bear. Unfortunately, on the last occasion this had happened the old man had been forced to caper until he had reached the point of exhaustion. He'd been capering when his heart had called it a day. Why, he'd died on the very spot Bream was standing on now. No one had told Bream about Andy. Miz Jenny, who might have done, had not been working for Jake at the time, and had probably not heard.

Jake, elbows propped upon the bar, had enjoyed the spectacle of a fearful Andy capering away. It had not even crossed his mind to haul out his shotgun and put an end to the entertainment, especially as it had been Travis Kentish who had forced Andy to dance. Jake was not a fool. Only a fool would lock horns with Tony Kentish, big shot rancher and pa to Travis. Like the rest of them, Jake had enjoyed the show. And when the old bum had fallen clutching his heart, Jake, like the rest of them, had not given a damn.

'Talk of the devil!' Jake exclaimed, perking up considerably when he saw who was swaggering through his batwings. 'Evening, Mr Travis,' Jake shouted loudly. Bream, he noticed, did not even look to see whom Jake was greeting.

Travis ignored the greeting, simply taking it as his due. 'Goddamnit, what an evening!' he exclaimed as he removed his waterproof. Carelessly he tossed the cape across a vacant table. His men, Shield and

Bainbridge, followed his lead. And all three swaggered towards the bar where a grinning Jake proclaimed that the first round of drinks was on the house.

Miz Jenny wondered why Jake was grinning.

'Bream, get on with your work, you no-account bum!' Jake bellowed, wanting to draw Travis's attention to the pot man who was working away steadily. 'From the way you are idling folk would think you were the saloon keeper not the saloon bum. Get them goddamn glasses gathered or you are out of a job!'

Miz Jenny sauntered casually towards Bream. 'Get out,' she whispered. 'I've got a nose for trouble and I reckon it is heading your way. Move casually towards the batwings then get as quick as you can.'

'Don't you worry, Miz Jenny,' Bream muttered. He had already realized the three galoots at the bar could be troublemakers. And he knew what Travis had done to old Andy. He'd heard talk. He kept his ears open!

'Travis is pure poison,' Miz Jenny hissed. 'I've seen his kind every town I've worked!'

Maybe he is, Bream thought. But as poison went he doubted whether Travis would measure up to Grandpa Bream. Yep, his grandpa had been poison and no doubt about it. Before he had died of natural causes the old man had slit a galoot's throat. The fool had belittled the old man and tried to take his wallet. No one had suggested the killing had been anything other than justified.

Bream was pleased that Miz Jenny seemed to be

worried about him. He considered her to be a mighty handsome woman and he had been wondering whether he could get enough cash together to ask Miz Jenny to go upstairs with him. Trouble was, he was uncertain as to how Miz Jenny might receive his proposal. She appeared to be an unpredictable female. She might agree to go up but she was just as likely to soundly box his ears for his presumption. Undoubtedly she was a woman of whom his grandpa would have approved.

'Get out of here, Bream,' Miz Jenny hissed. 'I don't want to see you dead.'

'Does that mean you'd. . . .'

'Yes. If you stay alive long enough. Now get!'

Bream moved towards the batwings. Miz Jenny had made his day, as they say.

Travis Kentish downed his third glass of whiskey in quick succession. The hard-eyed saloon woman Jenny had returned to the bar, he noted. She was a bit long in the tooth for him, he decided.

'She don't frighten!' Jake had already warned him. 'And I've heard it rumoured that she took a broken bottle to an *hombre* who backhanded her!

Travis liked women he could terrorize. He'd be able to handle Miz Jenny, no doubt about it. But he would not trouble himself with her. He was a young man after all and she sure was past her prime.

Old Andy's replacement, he noted, was a tall, thin beanpole of a galoot with scant fair hair. He decided he had found his punch-bag! The bum's luck had plumb run out.

He was gonna be the evening's entertainment.

'Get him over here,' Travis hissed at Jake, for the bum was heading for the batwings. Jake was more than happy to oblige. 'Get over here, Bream, you no-account bum,' he hollered 'I want a word with you. Move! I ain't got all night.'

The hair on Bream's neck prickled. His thoughts raced. Trouble was coming. And he needed a goddamn shooter to deal with it. True, he had a knife stowed in his boot, but a Peacemaker would be a darn sight more handy. He wanted this over with pretty damn quick. He approached the bar. It was plain to see that the young galoot intended to jut out his boot, thus causing him to trip. An apology would be demanded. And then rejected. It was an old ploy.

As he drew level with the young *hombre* called Travis, just as he had expected a fancy red boot was placed in his path. Neatly Bream avoided the boot. It was then Travis sprung the surprise. He had something else up his sleeve. Travis Kentish spat fair and square at Bream's face.

Jake sucked in his breath. Things were hotting up. From here on events would move fast.

'You damn bum, you've gotten in the way of my spit. What do you have to say?' Travis demanded truculently. He watched as the bum, using the sleeve of an old shirt, silently wiped spittle from his cheek. 'Beg my pardon and maybe I'll overlook your clumsiness this time.'

Bream glanced around the saloon. 'Would one of you gents be so kind as to lend me a Peacemaker?' he asked mildly.

'What the hell!' Travis exclaimed. Things were not

going to plan. And then he laughed. 'Let's see you dance. I want some entertainment. We all do!'

'And you're gonna get it,' Bream replied mildly.

'Goddamn it, give him a shooter!' Miz Jenny yelled. 'Before this young man, if you can call him that, decides to draw on an unarmed man.'

'Happy to oblige you, Miz Jenny.' A waddy from an outlying ranch unbuckled his gun belt and handed it to Bream, who slowly buckled the belt around his waist.

'You're a dead man,' Travis snarled as he watched in disbelief.

'Spittoon cleaners ain't hard to find,' Jake declared maliciously.

Bream flexed his right hand. He was a reasonable man. 'Now this don't have to end in gunplay,' he observed mildly. 'I don't want trouble. Let's put this misunderstanding behind us. What do you say?'

'You ain't no man. You're just a no-account bum. Get down and lick my boots and maybe I'll let you live.'

'And maybe you aim to kick out my teeth,' Bream rejoined. 'Now you folk had better get out of the line of fire.' Miz Jenny he noted approvingly, had already got down behind the bar. He eyed young Travis regretfully. 'I guess I'll have to blast you. I ain't dancing like poor old Andy. Shame on you, boy! And I ain't licking your boots. You've picked on the wrong man. Reach when you're ready.'

'You ain't getting no decent burial,' Travis roared, face red with rage. 'Coyote meat is all you are good for!'

Bream remained silent. There was little point in telling Travis he was a damn fool. And soon he was gonna be a dead fool.

'Bum!' Travis reached for his shooter.

Without conscious thought Bream reached for the borrowed .45. He drew the cumbersome weapon with practised ease, aimed and fired without even thinking about what he was doing, just instinctively aiming for the heart as he had been taught. He noted, in a detached kind of way, that Travis's shooter was just clearing its holster as his own bullet struck Travis in the chest. Blood spurted and Travis Kentish went down like a poleaxed steer.

To the left of Travis an *hombre* made the mistake of reaching. Bream, catching the movement, adjusted his position and fired. Bainbridge went down, the top of his head blasted clean away. Shield, who likewise had been about to reach, froze.

The stunned witnesses to the killings stayed silent. Today the sky might well have fallen. All hell was going to break loose. A man could not expect to kill Tony Kentish's boy and live. The vengeful rancher would deal out a terrible retribution.

'Wherever you go,' Shield croaked, 'Tony Kentish will find you. He'll have your hide. And that's a fact!'

Bream shrugged. He was not concerned. 'No it ain't,' he corrected. He eyed Jake coldly and found himself wishing Jake had reached for the shotgun kept behind the bar. 'Fact is, you'll be cleaning your own spittoons! I quit!'

CHAPTER THREE

Miz Maud was sitting on her porch. Her rocking-chair squeaked, a fact that irritated the large man standing beside her. Deliberately she rocked faster causing the squeaking to intensify.

'Leastways you could invite me into the parlour, Miz Maud,' he grumbled. 'I am here to propose after all!'

'You're here because you're after my ranch,' she snapped.

'You've never said a truer word, Miz Maud.' He laughed. 'And I aim to get it. There's a hard way and an easy way of doing it. See sense Miz Maud! Accept my proposal. Make us both happy.'

'I hear my neighbour has had his barn burnt to the ground!'

'Lucky he was not inside, I say.' Floyd Peters paused. 'Well, leastways he has seen sense. Old Archer is selling up. The papers have been signed. Now I would advise you to think carefully before declining my proposal, Miz Maud.'

'So you are giving me time to think. How generous!'

'Women find me agreeable,' he boasted.

'We'll have none of that kind of talk on my porch. Especially as we have company on the way. I believe the man is one of your hirelings!'

Floyd spun around, displeased to see that the approaching rider was indeed one of his crew. 'What the hell do you mean by disturbing me. I'm attending to an important matter.'

'Tony Kentish wants you to head for town!'

'I don't take orders from Kentish.'

'His boy has been blasted. He's dead. Gunned down by the bum who cleaned out the spittoons. He outdrew him. He outdrew Travis Kentish. And Travis was damn fast. His pa is getting a hunting party together. He aims to hunt down Bream, wants him taken alive, he says. He's out for vengeance.' Vernon paused, 'And there's worse. Seems like when Mrs Kentish heard the news she suffered a heart attack, upped and died. Not that Bream can be blamed for that I'd say, although Tony disagrees.'

'So Kentish is organizing a manhunt!'

'He sure as hell is. Tony says we can't have bums drifting in and murdering our own. He reckons you don't want to miss out on the fun, boss.'

Floyd Peters grinned. 'I sure as hell don't. I'm heading for town. You round up the hands, Vernon. I'll take ten along with me. They can draw straws to decide who rides with me.'

'Bream,' Miz Maud muttered. Her pa, she remembered, had spoken about a man named Bream. A loco killer was how he had described the man, but Kingdom, he had said, had always been respectful

31

towards women folk. Which was more than could be said for Floyd Peters.

'This Bream – is he an old man?'

'No, ma'am. He ain't middle-aged yet,' Vernon replied respectfully.

Was it possible the two men were related? Miz Maud closed her eyes. To survive, the man Bream would have to kill the whole damn lot of them, Floyd included. And if he were related to Kingdom Bream he would be more than capable of killing the whole darn bunch of them. At least, she hoped this would be the case.

'What an excellent idea. I will not need to send any of my men along. They won't be needed. I shall look forward to your return, Floyd.'

He looked at her suspiciously, then as realization dawned he roared with laughter. 'If you're thinking I ain't coming back, Miz Maud, then you're gonna have one hell of a disappointment. This is Eb Bream we are talking about, the saloon bum. Why, I heard tell his wife ran off and left him on account of him not being man enough to keep her. Now how about a farewell kiss, Miz Maud?'

'I'd rather spit in your eye,' she hissed. 'And I'll be praying Eb Bream sees to you good!'

'Don't count on it. And when I get back I'll see to you, Miz Maud, real good,' he promised with an evil leer. 'If you know what I mean!'

'I'll ride with you, Tony,' Jake declared. He glared at Miz Jenny. Bream had spent the night in town on account of the freak storm. Only a fool would ride out at night in that kind of weather. And Bream had

32

ordered Jake be locked away good in his own store-cupboard. Whilst he'd been locked away in that damn cupboard, Miz Jenny had been at it with Bream. He knew it. And he would have said so too, loud and clear, had not Miz Jenny begun cleaning her long nails with the point of a fancy knife. And all the while she had eyed Jake, smiling and declaring she could not abide men who liked to bad-mouth women, herself in particular. Jake, noting the expression in her eyes, had buttoned his lips. Miz Jenny was more than capable of knifing him, for she was a survivor, a woman who had survived the mining-camps and emerged unscathed! Now, hands on hips, she was watching the men cynically as they readied themselves to set out in pursuit of Eb Bream.

Bream had been on the look out for trouble when he left the saloon. But not one person had made a move to hinder him. No one had taken a pot shot at him. Folk were running scared. There was no one waiting outside to challenge him. Indeed the sidewalk was all but deserted.

'Well, I reckon someone will let Jake out of that goddamn cupboard,' he had told Miz Jenny, before adding: 'When I've dealt with any varmints who come after me I'll be coming back for you.' He had paused. 'If that's fine by you?'

Miz Jenny had shrugged. She had heard too many promises. 'You keep riding, Eb. I'm kinda fond of you. I've no wish to see you dead.'

'Then you don't object?'

'What I object to is you getting killed.'

33

'I'll be back, Miz Jenny. I'll be back, but I had better tell you I am a married man. Gracie ran off with a travelling salesman.'

'Thank the Lord you are married. Leastways it'll stop you getting down on one knee and making a darn fool of yourself.'

'I'd be honoured to do it, Miz Jenny, if I were free.'

'And I'd be obliged to refuse you, for I ain't never getting married. That's my one resolution. But I can't stop you coming back if you've a mind.'

They had left it at that. He had headed for the general store. It had yet to open up. Needing victuals and ammo, he had been forced to kick open the door and to help himself to whatever he needed. He made damn sure he took a plentiful supply of slugs. The boy's father would be coming after him. Miz Jenny had told him Tony Kentish would follow him to hell if needs be. Having got what he needed he squelched his way through the mud towards Howie's Livery Barn.

'Say!' the oldster exclaimed with a wide grin, 'you ain't related to old Kingdom Bream?'

'Yep. He was my grandfather,' Eb rejoined.

'And to think I took you for a bum!'

'I ain't my grandpa.'

'Come to think upon it I can see a resemblance,' the oldster mused. 'And sure as hell you've inherited his capabilities. And that means you stand a chance of surviving. Tony Kentish will follow you to hell and back now you have killed his no-account son. And be sure you get Floyd Peters. He'll be sure to tag along.'

'You old varmint. Why should I do you and this

Miz Maud a favour? And as I recall you aimed a gob at my boot and hit it too.'

'Well, I didn't realize you was related to Kingdom. And there ain't no reason to do me a favour other than Peters is poison. In his younger days he was a no-account bounty hunter. That's how he got his stake.'

'Saddle up my horse. I aim to ride.'

'Yes sir, Mr Bream,' Howie was respectful now. 'Your horse is saddled and ready. Now listen carefully, you watch out for Pedro. You know him, don't you. Leastways you have seen him around the saloon.'

'Yep.'

'Well he's aiming to dry-gulch you and claim the bounty.'

'What bounty?'

'The bounty Tony Kentish is gonna put on your head.'

'How the hell do you know this?'

'You know how it is. These young folk always seem to think us older ones ain't worth noticing. Fact is, he told Shield and I overheard. Shield now, he aims to lay low. He's keeping out of Kentish's way until it's safe for him to fork it out.'

'You tell Tony Kentish he ain't got no call to seek retribution, for right was on my side. Retribution gets men killed.' Bream paused, he sighed. 'Where the hell is Pedro. I reckon I'd best put the fear of hell into him. Damn fool. I don't reckon to kill folk unless I have to!'

'Holed up at the church. You'll need to ride by as

you fork it out. He aims to take a pot-shot. Pedro's great-aunt Juanita, she works for Kentish.' Howie paused, 'Kingdom would have done more than put the fear of hell into Pedro. He wouldn't have taken account of his youth.'

'Well I never wanted to follow in Kingdom's footsteps. Besides which, times are changing.'

'You tell that to Kentish!'

'Well I don't aim to talk to the man. Now listen, Howie, this is what I want you to do.'

After explaining to Howie he mounted and headed towards the outskirts of town and the brand new church built, so he'd heard, with Kentish money. He dismounted out of sight of the church and headed for the west side of the building. Pedro would be watching from the east windows ready to take a shot when he spotted his quarry. He drew his .45 and waited. Two shots rang out in quick succession and Howie was heard to yell that he had killed Eb Bream.

The young Mexican was drenched with sweat. His hands, in particular, were so slippery he could hardly hold his goddamn rifle. If he killed Bream he was sure of a job at the Kentish ranch. And the reward would be his. He had not expected to feel so queasy. And telling himself he was a tolerable shot and unlikely to miss did not help at all. When the shots rang out he almost jumped out of his skin, and he dropped his rifle. And then he heard Howie yelling how he had killed Eb Bream!

The riderless horse cantered down the muddy

track leading to the church and then stopped. And there it waited patiently, reins dangling.

'Goddamnit!' Pedro yelled. He came scrambling down from the upper gallery of the church. 'Goddamn Howie!' he yelled, rushing out of the church, his only thought being to ascertain whether Bream was well and truly dead. And he aimed to drive Howie off and claim the reward money for himself.

Bream felled him with a blow and gave him a boot for good measure as Pedro lay sprawled in the mud.

'You young varmint, so you aimed to dry-gulch me. Now crawl into that goddamn church.'

Pedro crawled, blubbering as he did so. Bream was not surprised. He gave Pedro another kick for good measure. 'Don't you ever again set out to kill a man who has done you no wrong. Are you listening, you no-account little varmint?'

'Yes sir,' Pedro blubbered.

'Well, I aim to make sure you remember. It might just save your hide!'

When Bream had finished inside the church he returned to his horse, mounted and prepared to ride. The greyness lying between night and day had lifted now. He guessed the polecats living in this town would be waiting for the big man himself, Mr Tony Kentish.

Musgrave's world had been turned upside down. The veteran ramrod had been with Tony Kentish from the day Tony had bought the ranch. Musgrave had never expected life to change so dramatically. And it had all happened in an instant. Travis was dead. Tony was demented with grief for his son. And Mrs Kentish had upped and died. Her body lay upstairs in the marital bed. Not that Tony was staying around to see her planted. The only thought in his mind was getting his hands on Eb Bream.

'I'm gonna make him beg for death,' Tony reiterated grimly.

Wisely, Musgrave had not pointed out that the potman could not be blamed for killing Travis. The fastest gun had won. That the bum had hauled iron like lightning was unexpected, but Travis had brought his fate upon himself by picking on the wrong man.

It had been William Child, the town pastor, who had brought the bad tidings. Musgrave did not care much for Child. With his long nose and sprouting whiskers Child always reminded Musgrave of a rat. Tony Kentish had howled like a mad dog and the sound had brought his wife down from her bed. And as soon as she had heard she had collapsed, clutching at her chest. Kentish had ignored his dead wife. It had been Child who had ordered the body to be taken upstairs.

Chaos ensued. Men were rounded up and they headed for town. They had found the place in an uproar, with folk milling around like headless chickens. Tony had headed straight for the undertakers and his dead son. It had been Musgrave who had freed Jake from the store cupboard. Jake had emerged cussing and whining that Bream had him covered before he could even think to reach for his shotgun. And why the hell Miz Jenny had not freed Jake, Musgrave did not know. But she soon told him!

'I don't interfere in men's business,' she had shrilled. 'It's healthier that way! Although it has been said I think like a man. Sure as hell I can fight as good as most. And sure as hell I can throw a blade better than any man I know. Ain't that so, Jake!'

'You go to hell, Miz Jenny,' Jake had growled.

It had been William Child rushing through the batwings who had brought news of what Bream had done with Pedro. And in a church of all places!

'Sacrilege!' Child cried, his face red with fury.

Musgrave, who had a peculiar sense of humour, had found it hard to keep a straight face. Just inside the church to the right of the door stood an imposing stone statue, a statue of Tony Kentish which carried the inscription CHURCH BENEFACTOR. No one had dared argue that perhaps the inside of the church was not the right place for the statue. And there, fastened to that statue, was Pedro, alive but frozen with fear, for Bream had looped wire around the boy to bind him to the statue. And on the stone floor Break had painted in white a single word: 'Fool'.

It was then that Musgrave began to experience misgivings. He was long in the tooth and wanted to die with his boots off. Eb Bream, so Musgrave believed, had been a humble telegraph clerk before he had become a town bum. Unexpectedly, Musgrave now found himself thinking of an old-time killer, one Kingdom Bream. If the two were related it explained a lot. Musgrave decided he had best find a way to extricate himself from this particular situation without being accused of turning yellow.

'Take a long hard look! That's the kind of man we are dealing with,' Tony was yelling.

'Well, he might have done a lot worse,' Howie, who had joined the group, observed. 'He might have taken Pedro's head off if he'd had a mind. Fact is I thought I had him.' Howie shrugged. 'He spared me on account of my age, so he said. Now hold still, boy, here come the wire cutters. You'll soon be free.'

'I'm riding with you, Mr Kentish. I am riding with you,' Pedro cried, finding his voice.

Howie turned away in disgust. Now Bream would have to kill the young idiot. Pedro had been given a second chance and thrown it away.

Bream rode west towards the mountains. He whistled softly. The rain had stopped, and he felt good. He had a good start. An idea was gnawing away at him. Indirectly, it involved Miz Jenny.

'Hell, Bream, when I can get around to it I aim to pay Willard Bliss another visit,' Miz Jenny had been wont to say as she lounged against the bar. 'The varmint slammed the door in my face and Bessie yelled out she wanted me gone, for she was a respectable woman now,' Miz Jenny had said. 'And that sure as hell hurt Bream for Bessie and me, we go back.' She would pause. 'And I never did care for Willard Bliss. That polecat makes my flesh creep. There's something that just ain't right about Willard Bliss.'

'And where is this Willard Bliss?' Bream had asked.

Miz Jenny had given him directions. Eb intended to ask Miz Jenny out one day for a buggy ride. They could call upon Bessie Bliss, he would say. But he never had. And now of all times he felt a sudden urge to call upon Bessie Bliss. It made no sense. He was running for his life but, goddamn it, he was going to call upon Bessie Bliss. It would cost him time. Folk had told him often enough that he was a fool, so why not behave like one!

Unaware that an unwanted caller was on the way Willard Bliss was cooking. Chicken soup with dumplings bubbled on the stove. And he had made apple pie laced with sugar. He loved to cook. But not for himself! There was no way Bessie could ever up and leave him now!

He'd had his eye on Bessie from the first time he had seen her plump, smiling face. Bessie, he had seen, was manageable and none too bright. Every day since he had met her he had told her how special she was. And he had taken her out of the saloon and married her. These days his Bessie was one special woman.

As Bream cautiously approached Willard's homestead a small half-starved mutt ran out to greet him. And then, tail between its legs, made itself scarce beneath the porch, just as Willard, cradling his rifle appeared at the front door.

'What the hell do you want?' he demanded without preamble.

'How's Miz Bessie?' Bream enquired.

Willard spat. 'What's it to you?' he demanded truculently.

41

'Miz Jenny sends her regards. She has asked me to look in on her old friend. My name is Eb Bream.'

'My Bessie is a respectable married woman now. She wants nothing to do with the old whore!'

Bream curbed his rage. 'You call Miz Jenny an old whore again and you'll regret it. And as for Miz Bliss, well she can tell me to go to hell herself. I won't take offence!'

'You go to hell, Bream,' Bliss snarled. 'I'm telling you to get!'

'I want to see her, Willard,' Bream replied, thinking that Willard looked a mite shifty. This suggested the man had something to hide. Maybe he'd been beating up Bessie and wanted to hide the fact.

'I'm telling you to get! I know you. You're the bum that cleans the spittoons. That's how you know Miz Jenny. Filth, the pair of you!'

'Bum or not I aim to say good day to Miz Bessie before riding on.'

At that, Willard started to raise his rifle. Bream had been expecting Bliss to make a move. Although why the man should he did not know! Instinctively he grabbed for his Peacemaker. And then, without conscious thought, he shot Willard Bliss through the chest. He regretted it instantly but Willard had not given him a choice. Willard had aimed to kill him, but why?

He found himself recalling a time from his youth. Grandma Bream had sent Grandpa to check out a neighbour. Now Grandpa had been assured all was well but he had insisted on seeing the woman for himself. He had found her black and blue. There had been a confrontation with the husband and Grandpa had blasted the man. And had that woman thanked him? No, not at all. She had tried to kill Kingdom herself. He had wrestled the gun away from her and had lived in fear of his life until she had moved back East. 'A man can't win,' he had griped. And now Bream, recalling this cautionary tale, half-expected a deranged Bessie Bliss to emerge from the homestead, foaming at the mouth with a gun in her hand, intent upon blasting him.

Peacemaker at the ready, he kicked in the home-stead door. 'I'm a friend of Miz Jenny,' he hollered. 'Don't be afraid' He wondered how he was going to break the news that he had just blasted Willard.

'Willard!' a voice called. 'Willard!'

Bream kicked open the bedroom door. What he saw caused him to back away, scarcely able to believe his eyes.

Bessie Bliss lay on the bed. She was a behemoth. Her legs, bulging against the tentlike garment she thankfully wore, were like tree-trunks. Fat hung from her in rolls. She was so fat he reckoned she could barely walk. And the room stank as well.

'How'd you get like this?' he croaked.

'Willard! He's been feeding me. But I don't mind! What have you done to my Willard?'

'Nothing he don't deserve. The varmint has fattened you like a hog. And you say you don't mind!' Bream collected himself. 'Well, I reckon I have done you a favour Miz Bliss. You tell them that come after me to fetch Miz Jenny. You were friends once. I reckon she'll help you out. Sure as hell there ain't no one to feed you now.' Shaking his head and closing his ears to her howls Bream retreated. Sure as hell, Willard's monstrous secret would be disclosed. He put Willard's pot of chicken soup down for the dog. But he ate the fresh-baked pie. And then he left. He had no choice. In any event the so-called posse on his trail would discover Bessie Bliss sooner or later.

'You see what kind of man we're dealing with! Filth! The lowest of the low!' Tony Kentish was practically foaming at the mouth. 'He's blasted an innocent man and then left him to fester!'

'Damn flies.' Musgrave did not attempt to swat at the flies swarming around the remains of Willard Bliss. 'Good riddance. We've all seen what that polecat has done to Bessie. Why, he was loco I'd say.'

'It's gonna rain again,' Tony squinted at the dark clouds rolling across the sky. 'We'll spend the night at the Bliss place. You two men,' he jerked his head, 'see to the horses. We've run them hard.'

'I won't be riding with you tomorrow,' Musgrave announced.

'The hell you say!'

'Fact is me and Bessie were acquainted way back. I feel obliged to look out for her. Why, the woman can't hardly walk thanks to that polecat Willard!' Musgrave forced a grin. 'I reckon you don't need me to run down Bream. He's a no-account bum, you said so yourself. There ain't no need for any of us to be afraid of Eb Bream, spittoon-cleaner. Ain't that so, Jake?'

Jake did not respond. He merely spat. Which

could have been taken either way.

'You're damn right I don't need you. You're a yellow-belly.' Kentish reacted predictably. 'And a halo don't set right on your head. It's this two-bit ranch you're interested in, not that thing inside.'

'Bessie ain't no thing,' Musgrave rejoined mildly, highly relieved that he was out of it. Instinct told him the hunting party would come to grief.

Tony spat. 'You're long in the tooth. I was aiming to replace you in any event.'

'Goddamn, will you look at that,' Ronald Bagshot exclaimed as Bessie staggered on to the porch.

'Jenny,' she wheezed. 'I want Jenny.'

'Of course you do,' Musgrave soothed. 'Young Vernon here will ride back to town first thing tomorrow. He'll fetch Miz Jenny.'

'I ain't going,' young Vernon exclaimed. 'I ain't missing the fun!'

Musgrave shrugged. 'Fair enough.' He'd been endeavouring to save Vernon's hide. The young man had a widowed ma, after all. 'Let's get you back inside, Bessie.' He took her arm, trying not to flinch as he did so.

'Let's all get inside,' Floyd Peters suggested. 'And I'll thank you to keep your lip buttoned, Musgrave. Vernon works for me.' He paused. 'If that heap of lard falls on you, you're done for in any event.'

Raucous laugher greeted this remark. Musgrave ignored the lot of them. He was just glad he was out of the chase. He'd stay safe. And it was true, Bessie could not be left. Furthermore, he had always wanted a spread of his own. Willard's place wasn't much but it was better than ramrodding for an ungrateful cuss such as Kentish.

'I will fetch Miz Jenny,' William Child, the town preacher stated as they trooped into the Bliss home. 'It's my Christian duty.' Unused to sitting a horse Child felt as though his behind were on fire. His place was in town. He should never have volunteered to join the manhunt. But like many of them he had got carried away. To his relief no one challenged his offer or accused him of being yellow, a privilege that went with being town preacher. 'But what of Willard? He needs to be buried.'

'Hell, it's just got to wait. Friend Musgrave can attend to it. We ain't shovelling mud in the rain,' Kentish exclaimed. 'At least the rain will discourage those pesky flies.'

With the men inside and the place quiet the dog crept out from beneath the porch. It was hungry once more. Giving a growl it took hold of Willard's outstretched hand and began to gnaw.

CHAPTER FOUR

Bream spent the night huddled beneath his tarp. Upon reflection he wasn't sorry that he had killed Willard Bliss. The varmint deserved it! The man was clearly mad.

He breakfasted on cold jerky. He was unable to build a fire and brew coffee, which had made him realize just how dependent he had become upon his morning brew of strong black coffee. He felt like a bear with a sore head. And now the sun had come out and his wet clothes were steaming. And worse, his bones were aching. Years of town living had made him unsuited to life on the trail.

Faint but distant he heard the shots, confirmation that Kentish was hell bent on retribution. Bream scratched his chin. Kentish would have to be killed. There was no other way, not if he wanted to keep on living. The distant gunfire got him moving without further delay. He was in unfamiliar territory without any choice but to keep going, and an uninviting canyon lay ahead. If he doubled back he might run into the varmints. Face to face, outnumbered, he wouldn't stand a cat's chance in hell.

As he rode on his anger grew. Those bastards who were in pursuit would be enjoying themselves; the thrill of the chase, he supposed. Personally he could see nothing thrilling in hunting a man down to kill him, and not with a clean shot either. Miz Jenny had warned him what to expect from Kentish. A string of curses left his lips as he rounded the bend in the trail ahead, for a solid wall of rock reared up before him.

He patted his horse, to comfort himself more than the horse. The horse wasn't in any danger of being skinned alive. It looked as though his luck had run out, but Eb Bream had never believed in luck. He could not go back. It would be a foolish and potentially lethal move. He wiped his brow. He knew what he had to do. The trouble was he could never be a boy again, without a thought that things could go wrong. The young Eb Bream had never worried about splitting his skull open or breaking his back.

'Hell!' he exclaimed, 'I'm growing old.' But if he didn't get moving it was unlikely he'd grow a day older than he was now.

Old Indian Joe slept with the horses in the stable. Folks often wondered why Floyd had kept old Joe around, for Floyd was not an altruistic man. Well, now they knew. Old Joe was the best damn tracker ever. None of them would admit it but without him it would have been mighty hard, maybe impossible, to track Eb Bream.

Joe did not care whether they ran down the hunted man. He himself did not intend to be in at the kill, if indeed there was a kill! He was pretty damn sure that by the end of the hunt many of these fools would be dead. Kingdom Bream had been crazy, far crazier than Kentish or Peters. Anyone raised by Kingdom would have been taught how to kill, and kill well.

Joe clamped a cigar given to him by Floyd between toothless gums. He pointed.

'You've got him, boss. There ain't no way out.' Joe then dismounted and proceeded to wrap a blanket around his scrawny shoulders.

'What the hell!' Kentish exclaimed angrily.

'If Joe says we've got him, we've got him,' Peters clarified. 'What's he's telling us is that Eb Bream has ridden into one of the box canyons hereabouts. Now all that's left is to flush him out. Joe knows he ain't needed. He's gonna sit here and smoke a cigar or two whilst we do what's needed to be done. He's a mighty fine tracker. I keep him around to run down any wideloopers who mess with my steers. Not that we see many hereabouts. I reckon they know what's in store for them.'

'You're goddamn right they do.' Kentish paused. 'Any of you men that has got a squeamish stomach had best stay put.' He spat. 'Hanging is too good for Bream. I aim to douse him in kerosene and set him on fire. I can't bring my boy back but I can avenge him. Speak up if anyone has anything to say about the matter.'

Gregory Bagshot was a fool. Being on a manhunt had filled him with exhilaration. He himself had been mortally afraid of falling foul of Travis Kentish but all that was forgotten now.

'Goddamn right you are, Mr Kentish. Goddamn right. We're with you all the way!' He then discharged his rifle once more into the air.

Tony Kentish snapped. 'Goddamn fool.' He struck Gregory full across the face. 'Goddamn fool. If he's in there, thanks to you he knows now how close behind we are. Goddamn fool. Ronnie!' he rounded on Gregory's pa, 'ain't you taught these boys of yours a goddamn thing?'

Ronald would have liked to blast Tony there and then. His boys Gregory and Guy had stampeded him into joining the manhunt.

'Me and my boys will be leaving now, Mr Kentish,' he rejoined with a mildness he did not feel. 'We ain't needed. Come on, boys, we're heading home to your ma.'

'Well I ain't going,' Guy, the younger, declared. 'I aim to see that beanpole bum.'

'And I ain't quitting neither.' Gregory wiped his face with the back of his sleeve, aware that his nose was bleeding.

Ronald Bagshot clamped a pipe between his yellowed teeth. He stared long and hard at his boys. 'I'm your pa and I am ordering you home.' His voice shook with emotion.

'You go to hell, you old fool,' Gregory yelled, shocking the men he was riding with.

'Looks like you've been told, Ronnie, looks like you've been told.' Kentish relished Ronald's humiliation.

'It's as clear as day who wears the apron in your

50

house.' Jake could not resist the insult.

Ronald Bagshot glared at his boys. The truth of the matter was he did not much care for either one of them. They were unlovable varmints. He nodded.

'I'll see you boys back at the ranch.' Without another word he turned his horse around and headed for home. They were beyond his help. He felt sick in the pit of his stomach. He wanted no part of this. Why, his boys hardly seemed human now, nor did the rest of 'em.

'Let's flush him out,' Tony suggested to Guy. 'If you're man enough you can light the match!'

'Yes sir, you can count on me, Mr Kentish,' Guy replied. He had never before felt so alive and so powerful. He felt he was somebody and Eb Bream, town bum, was nobody!

Bream unsaddled his horse, removed the bridle and turned the animal free. His hands, he was glad to see, remained steady. They did not tremble. He eyed the canyon wall noting with relief that although it was sheer it was not smooth. There were niches and stunted bushes sprouting from cracks in the rock face, hand- and toe-holds which he reckoned would get him safely to the top. Making this climb success-fully was the only chance he had to save his hide. And when it came to climbing he was not a novice. Even a telegraph clerk had time off. Every Sunday when Gracie headed for church Bream had headed out into the countryside and he had there indulged his two pursuits, target practice and climbing. But the climbs he had undertaken had been ones he had considered safe. It had kept him sane, for his wife had never stopped nagging him.

'You ain't meant to climb. You ain't no goddamn monkey,' his grandpa had hollered. With hindsight Eb realized the old man had been mortally afraid his grandson was gonna have a real serious fall.

'I ain't never seen a real live monkey,' Bream muttered as he commenced his climb. 'Maybe Miz Jenny and me could travel around and find ourselves a real live monkey swinging from the trees,' he muttered. 'Yep. That's what we'll do!' Not that he gave a damn about monkeys: muttering to himself kept him from thinking about falling. He put Kentish and the hunting party from his mind. He forced himself to move slowly and with the utmost care. He was good at this. And sure as hell none of the varmints would be climbing up after him.

Gregory Bagshot was gabbing once more. 'I aim to get myself one of Bream's ears,' he declared. 'Before we burn him. I reckon to keep a token just to remind myself. I never did like Eb Bream.'

'You do that!' Kentish spat. 'Whoever wants a keepsake can help himself!'

He's loco, Floyd Peters decided. Grief had driven Kentish crazy. And the sooner this was over the better. He had business with Miz Maud, pleasurable business.

'Hell, I can't wait to see the look on Miz Jenny's face when she hears what happened to Eb Bream,' Jake declared maliciously. 'What the hell did she see in him anyhow?' He glanced around at his companions. 'Damned if I know!'

'Well, there ain't no understanding women,' a waddy declared, the observation raising a few laughs. The men were nervous and not all of them agreed with what Kentish had in store for Bream. But without exception they all wanted it over and done with. 'But you tread wary around Miz Jenny. She ain't right in the head!'

'He's cornered like a rat!' Brindissi, the portly hotel-keeper, declared. He was sweating profusely and wishing he wasn't here. He'd only come along to spite his wife. He had wanted to worry her! Well, he intended to lag behind. He wasn't going to be in at the kill. He had never thought they would catch up with their quarry.

The fact that Bream was cornered like a rat in a trap was making a difference. Men who had been beginning to flag were now filled with renewed vigour. The townsmen, unaccustomed to hours in the saddle for the most part, managed to rally. Tiredness was forgotten and the euphoria increased when a riderless horse trotted into sight.

'That's Bream's nag,' Walters, a grizzled veteran, declared. He felt a vague unease. 'Eb Bream is gonna be making his last stand,' he declared, more to reassure himself than anything.

'If he's got any sense he'll blast himself,' Jake muttered.

A waddy guffawed and then Jake declared Eb Bream had no sense at all for the fool had been taken with Miz Jenny!

'My heart!' Brindissi clutched his chest. If Eb Bream was gonna make his last stand, Brindissi had suddenly decided not to be part of it.

'Get the hell out of here. You bum! You turn my stomach,' Kentish snarled. 'You ain't got the stomach for what's ahead, I can see.' He paused. 'I'll lead us in. You men can follow if you have a mind. Those of you who have more stomach for justice than this damned hotel-keep, that is!'

'Yeah, get back to town you yellow-belly!' a waddy exclaimed.

Brindissi's face turned red. His large belly, which hung over his belt, rumbled. He was missing his food. '*Sí*,' he responded, '*Sí*.' He turned away as someone yelled out that Brindissi had more stomach than the rest of them put together. Hoots of laughter greeted this quip.

'We're better off without him,' Walters cackled, wondering maliciously whether Brindissi would be able to find his way back to town. Brindissi was wondering the very same thing but dared not voice his fear. Not that any of these men would give a damn if he perished, lost and alone. Goddamnit, what was he doing here with them any way? He had no quarrel with Eb Bream. And his wife had cried and begged him not to go!

Peacemaker drawn, Tony Kentish led them into the canyon. At this moment he did not care any more if he lived or died. All he cared about now was getting Eb Bream, preferably alive. 'Shoot to disable,' he yelled, 'I want that bum alive. Do you hear? I'll blast the man who kills him myself. He's gonna burn. He's gonna burn for what he did to my Travis. And his ma,' he added belatedly.

*

His breath escaping in raw gasps, Bream hauled himself over the rim and on to firm ground. His back was plastered with sweat. Once he had almost fallen. He had been able to imagine lying there helpless, his back broken, at the mercy of Tony Kentish. Just imagining this plight had fuelled his resolve. He could make this climb. And now he had!

Bellying down, he surveyed the canyon floor below, and then set about unwrapping his rifle. He had kept it dry during the downpour last night. It had to be done. He took a deep breath, several in fact; shooting men down without warning filled him with revulsion, but these varmints had allied themselves with Kentish who was after his hide. Kentish was the key, he reckoned. If he could take out Kentish then it would be over

He could see them now, coming into view, and he recognized most of them: men he had seen whilst he'd been emptying spittoons and cleaning floors, men he had exchanged a few words with. What the hell were they doing riding with Kentish? Too bad for them! To save himself he'd kill the whole darn bunch of them without a qualm.

Jake was there. Now that was expected. And beside Jake, just in the lead, a man who had to be Tony Kentish. Bream sighted his rifle and squeezed the trigger, and as the shot reverberated the hunting party scattered.

'Well, it was a long shot,' Bream muttered philosophically.

'He's up the top!' Floyd Peters hollered, taking care not to emerge from behind the rocks he'd hidden behind.

'It don't seem possible.' Walters shook his head. 'That man must be part goat. Probably that's why his wife upped and left,' he concluded with a guffaw.

Others joined in the laughter but not Tony Kentish. 'Shut your goddamn mouths. This ain't a joke,' he screamed as control momentarily left him.

The laughter stopped abruptly. Walters clamped a pipe between his gums.

'We're gonna get him. We're gonna get him,' Floyd vowed. 'Old Indian Joe will find a way up and then we will have him!' And then he began to yell: 'We're gonna get you, Eb Bream. We're gonna get you!'

'You bastard, Bream, you bastard!' Tony Kentish yelled. 'You're gonna burn. You're gonna burn!'

Rosie Hobbs was down to her last dollar. She was headed for the town of Kentish when she saw the man, a fat man with a domelike head, bald on top, just sitting on a fallen tree, his horse tethered to a branch. Rosie approached with caution.

Brindissi stared at the weather-lined face of the approaching female in some surprise. It was not every day one saw a lone female dressed as a man and packing a Peacemaker.

'Don't try anything. I'll blast you if you so much as twitch,' she warned without preamble.

'I'm a happily married man with ten children,' he rejoined, much put out by her insinuation.

'Well, you might be happy but I reckon your wife

56

ain't!' she quipped.

'That is only your opinion.'

Hobbs shrugged. She would not argue the point. 'So what are you doing out here?' A fool question, she realized, for he immediately began to tell her what he was doing out here. In the space of twenty or so minutes Rosie heard all about Tony Kentish, Eb Bream and everyone else for that matter.

'So what are you doing out here?' he at last enquired.

'I'm heading for Kentish. I need a job. Know anyone who might hire me?'

To her surprise he nodded. 'Miz Maud only has two men. One is old and one is stupid. You take me to town and I will give you free meals and a room at my hotel if Miz Maud does not hire you. He paused. 'Floyd Peters wants Miz Maud's ranch. If he gets back no job for you!'

Hobbs nodded. 'You're desperate, ain't you! You don't know how to get back to town! Well, it's a deal. You're a man of your word, I hope. I blast them that crosses me.'

Bream knew the varmints would backtrack. Sooner or later they would find a way up to high ground. But it would take them time. Northwards across an expanse of scrub were hills and, as Bream knew, a man could lose himself in hill country. And crossing the vast expanse of spiked scrub would slow his pursuers down considerably.

Anger churned inside him. All he had ever sought to do was to avoid trouble. Indeed folk had always regarded him as a likeable man.

'You're a likeable man but so darn boring,' Gracie, his wife had whined. He wondered what she would think now, here he was running for his life. Bream cursed softly. To save himself he would of necessity have to kill the whole darn bunch of them. He had no choice. The likeable *hombre* was set to become plain unlikeable.

He headed for the scrub. Spiked mesquite and chaparral abounded. He'd have to be damn careful, for these thorns could take out an eye. High above the storm-clouds had rolled away and the sky was an unblemished blue; a good day to die! What a goddamn thought and what a goddamn shame he'd failed to hit Tony Kentish. The distance had been just a little too far. His legs were hurting like hell. He was out of condition. He had been too busy cleaning spittoons and feeling sorry for himself to keep himself in shape.

A yellow-headed bird flew across his path. To his left came the sound of movement. He froze. The steer, horns long and viciously pointed, crossed his path before moving away into the scrub. He heaved a sigh of relief. These rogue steers, critters that had gone wild, could be lethal. He knew of two unfortunate waddies who had been gored to death by these cantankerous critters. Not that he could blame them seeing as they'd originally been destined to end up on a dinner-plate.

From time to time he stooped, taking care to avoid the thorns, and carefully picked up and pocketed a jagged stone. He was handy when it came to hurling these missiles. A forcefully hurled stone striking the head could kill a man. He'd seen it done once!

'Damn fools,' he muttered, referring to his pursuers. The whole darn bunch of them had been seized with an obsessive madness. That damn fool young Pedro had tagged along, and he had recognized the two Bagshot boys. Raising his canteen to his lips he sipped tepid water. It would not be easy for them to track him through thick scrub. But he was not fool enough to think Kentish would give up the chase.

Indian Joe did not need to be told the men had failed. Their expressions said it for them. And the mood was ugly now. He sensed it. Joe stood up. His bones ached. He wanted to sleep.

'You damn bag of bones,' Kentish yelled, seizing Joe by the shirt, 'You get us up top pretty damn quick.' He waved his fist in front of Joe's nose.

'Sure thing,' Joe grunted. They were laughing now, laughing at him, even boss Peters. His brow furrowed. It was bad country up top, real bad country but no one wanted to hear what he had to say. He was expected to keep his goddamn mouth shut. And so he would, but he was not venturing into bad countrt. Instinct told him these half-crazed men would shoot him out of hand if he said anything about wanting to quit. He clamped a cigar between his gums, kicked his horse into movement and headed out, back the way they had come. He knew where he was going, knew just the trail that would take them up top.

'I'm counting on you, Joe,' Tony bellowed. 'You let me down and I'll have your hide. Savvy?'

'Me savvy,' Joe grunted. And they would too, before this was over.

Bream kept moving, aware that any gashes he got would attract the pesky flies which always swarmed when they homed in on blood. He kept moving while the light lasted and then stretched out on the hard ground. His legs were chronically aching and a blister on his toe throbbed continuously. He drifted, half-asleep and half-awake, sometimes fantasizing about Miz Jenny, sometimes thinking of his runaway wife. In his head he heard her shrill voice:

'It's all your own fault. Don't you expect any sympathy, Eb Bream. You ain't going to get any!'

He sat up with a grunt. Dawn was breaking. A new day was here. He lurched to his feet. Goddamn it, why couldn't Gracie have run off sooner. If Gracie ever came looking for him he would be the one doing the running. Stretching, he eyed the wooded hills. They were as far away as ever. Looking down at his feet he willed them to move. And he found himself wondering about Tony Kentish and the hunting party.

As Joe made a pretence of searching for a way up top the insults came fast and furious as the frustration of the men grew. They were on edge now. This hunt had not proved to be the picnic they had thought it was going to be. Floyd Peters had been heard to laugh good-naturedly at some of the insults directed at Joe. But there was nothing good-natured about it at all. Like a pack of mad dogs, they were liable to turn on their weakest member. Himself!

'You find us a way up or you are a dead man,' Kentish bellowed.

'You ain't nobody, Joe,' a waddy shouted. 'Just Floyd's pet dog. And the way I see it you're an old dog and no goddamn use! It's time you were put out of your misery!'

Joe stopped. Turning his head he regarded the sullen faces, nodded and then pointed. 'We go get Bream. We take the quickest way, lose no time.' And then Joe started up the barely visible track, knowing they would follow as he made the ascent look easy.

Kentish took the lead, followed by Peters and Jake. Behind Jake came the Bagshot boys and Pedro. Walters led the ranch hands and the men from town rode last. They were about half-way up the steep incline when it began to dawn on Tony Kentish that it would have been wiser to lead the horses up. The track was becoming ever more narrow as it rose sharply, loose shale beginning to slither downwards as it was disturbed. Kentish found himself perspiring with unease.

Mathew Archer's horse balked. Archer dug in his silver-star spurs, an instinctive reaction that defeated itself with the horse sidestepping and toppling. Archer fell with a howl of sheer terror, oblivious of the chain of events he had set in action.

Men and horses at the tail end of the hunting party went down like cards. Kentish cursed as the townsmen went down, men and horses screaming in

61

pain and terror.

'Leave them be!' he yelled as those who were spared made to go to the help of the injured. 'There ain't nothing we can do. We can't tote 'em back to town. We've got to get after Bream. If we stop now we'll lose him.'

'I can't move my legs,' Peter Holt screamed in terror. Mathew Archer lay near by, dead, crushed beneath his horse.

'Vernon, you get on back down. You fetch help. Those of us who have made it safely up are gonna go on after Bream.' Peters eyed Joe suspiciously, but the tracker remained impassive.

'I reckon I'll stay with the injured,' Walters decided. 'It's my duty as I see it. Besides which I'm long in the tooth and may slow you down.' He'd had enough. It was a goddamn scene of carnage below, with men and horses down, horseflesh threshing with legs broken, men unconscious, men dead, men so shocked they could scarce move. Walters had been around. He knew that goddamn Kentish ought to have treated Joe with respect. This was the result. The wily old tracker would have known that this would happen; only experienced horsemen should have attempted the death-trail. With Joe playing tricks Walters aimed to quit the chase. 'I'll put the injured critters out of their misery. Horses, that is. It's gotta be done.'

'We go,' Joe urged. 'Get that goddamn Bream.'

High above, buzzards were already circling. Walters shut his ears to the cries of pain. Vernon was already forking it back to town. Walters drew his

62

Peacemaker and put the nearest downed horse out of its misery, having first hobbled his own critter. If Vernon did not return with help Walters aimed to fork it out. It was as clear as day that from here on the hunting party were going to be dogged with bad luck. Walters was glad he was no longer part of it. He guessed he owed Joe a vote of thanks. If his hunch were right Joe would soon be removing himself from the vicinity of the ill-fated hunting party.

'Get the tarps up,' he grunted. 'And get them that's hurt bad under the tarps.' He paused. 'There ain't nothing we can do, save try and splint a few broken limbs.' He eyed Peter Holt; the poor bastard would never walk again. He guessed that when Holt realized the situation he would blast his own brains out.

Significantly, those who could were now beginning to curse Tony Kentish, saying what Eb Bream had done was between him and Kentish. Walters spat. Damn fools! A manhunt was no picnic. They ought to have known it. But that was townfolk for you. And for a townsman, Bream was doing more than fine! And then he understood. Memory surfaced! *Kingdom Bream*! Walters clicked his fingers. The damn fools were hunting Kingdom Bream's grandson!

CHAPTER FIVE

To his surprise a trail of sorts seemed to be leading the way through the scrub. This had made his progress easier. Even so, by the time he reached the sloping hills he was in a bad way. He was limping badly. His legs were like jelly. His rumbling stomach would easily have revealed his whereabouts to any one close enough to hear its churning and gurgling. But thank the Lord, he was alone. There was no sign of his pursuers, or anyone else for that matter. But his unease was growing.

He could scarce believe his luck had changed when he spotted the rabbit. It sat there, small and scrawny and young. His next meal if he could bag it. He cursed beneath his breath. His arms felt stiff and useless. His fingers closed over the stone in his pocket. He dare not risk a shot, not wanting to alert the hunting party or anyone else for that matter to his presence. He hefted the stone, praying that years of idle practice would bear fruit. It did. The stone whacked the rabbit's head fair and square with a soft thud that felled it instantly.

Licking his lips, he headed for the rabbit, but froze as he stooped to retrieve it, for right by the fallen rabbit an object stuck from the soil. And that object was clearly a finger. A woman had been buried here. That clearly signified that others were about and he was not fool enough to think that if he encountered them he would be met with a friendly reception. Squatting down, with the aid of his blade he carefully scraped away the soil, just enough to reveal the whole hand. The nails, he noted, were broken. Had she put up a fight then, before she died? He reckoned that she had. More to the point, she had been recently buried. How the hell had she died? Who had killed her? What kind of varmints was he likely to encounter. His skin prickled. He expected a slug to hit him at any moment now. It did not. He replaced the earth, leaving the finger exposed as it had been before. His curiosity as to how she had met her death must remain unsatisfied. To determine how she had died he would have to dig her out, and he was not so crazy that he would embark upon such an undertaking with his own life at stake.

There was every chance that, as he proceeded, he would encounter whoever was responsible for this freshly buried female. The trail of sorts that he had found and followed through the scrub was not accidental. It had been made over time and it was used regularly enough to keep it open. Damnit it, he could not risk a fire. His meal must be eaten raw. And he damn well hoped the raw meat would not cause his stomach to cramp up.

Sheltering beneath the trees he skinned the rabbit. And his stomach gagged as he forced down still-warm flesh. He forced his jaws to move and swallowed with effort, thinking drily that Gracie's burnt breakfasts had come in useful after all, for they were proving to be darn good training. Yes sir, if he could get her breakfasts down he could manage this rabbit. And when he came to think about Gracie, why it was as plain as the nose on his face that she had been burning his food deliberately.

He also became aware that he stank like a polecat. But he guessed his pursuers would be in the same predicament, and whoever was holed up out here doubtless stank as well. So he hoped, or they would be able to smell him a mile away.

Having eaten and concealed the remains he cautiously scouted around. Soon he hit upon another trail that led upwards. Instinct, however, told him to steer clear of that goddamn trail. He would skirt around it. It would take longer but it would be a whole heap safer. If there were an outlaw band holed up ahead there would be look-outs posted, and maybe a few surprises along the way.

Munro regarded the stretch of scrub that lay between the hunting party and the hills with disbelief. He wiped his brow, thinking the fact was that most of the time folk in town kinda forgot Eb Bream existed. The man had kept himself to himself, preferring not to pass the time of day with casual acquaintances, nor had the man ever been seen to drink alcohol whilst he had been in town. It was a puzzle to Munro why a man as fast at hauling iron as Eb Bream had been cleaning spittoons. Nor was it Bream's fault that Travis Kentish had made on hell of a mistake.

'That damn mad dog is leading us one hell of a chase,' Jake grunted as he produced a whiskey-bottle. He took a slug and wiped the back of his mouth.

Munro made his decision. 'I ain't going in there!' he exclaimed.

'What are you saying?' Floyd growled, for Munro was one of his men.

'I quit,' Munro replied bluntly. 'Fact is I've got a bad feeling about all of this.'

'You're yellow!' Floyd accused.

'Well, maybe I am. But it's a fact Lady Luck has left us,' Munro rejoined. 'If she was with us we would have had Bream by now. I ain't partial to hill country. I'm heading back to town.'

His boss spat. 'Have it your own way, but don't be around when I get back. And if you make the mistake of stopping by to pick up your goddamn wages you are a dead man. Same applies if you trespass on my land.'

'Fair enough,' Munro agreed, turning away. He did not give a damn about money owing. He wanted to live!

'Anyone else with a yellow streak?' Kentish yelled angrily.

Silence greeted his question.

'Good. When we get back to town you boys can drink until you can't stand up. On me! I'll even pay for the whores as well. You deserve it! I won't deny it's gonna be a long haul before we run down Bream.

67

The bastard will be hoping we'll give up.'

Loud cheers and raucous comments greeted these words. Munro, riding away, heard the cheers. He thinned his lips. Damn fools, he thought, for they had yet to realize that Bream was poison.

'Get moving, you old buzzard!' Kentish addressed old Joe.

'We'd best rest and eat,' Floyd interrupted. 'Once Joe gets moving we'll go like lightning. There just ain't no stopping him once he gets the scent.'

'Let's hope so,' a rancher muttered. 'We're ranching men, after all. We can't afford to be away too long.'

Bream heard the distant voices, just as dusk began to fall.

'I ain't going back. I ain't going back.' The voice was high and shrill: a child, he reckoned. There was more than one of them, so it seemed. As luck would have it he'd spotted the hollowed trunk of an old tree that lay some way from the trail he was skirting. He crawled inside, determined to stay put until he knew what the hell was going on. He felt no urge to discover whether these young ones needed help. They had no business in this wilderness.

'It's getting dark. We've gotta put the tarp up.' The boy sounded desperate.

Bream was not fool enough to emerge from his hiding-place to offer assistance.

'Grandma will get you anyway.' There was a pause. 'And then you'll be for it!' The second speaker was a girl.

Goddamn little varmints had better not discover his hiding-place. And by the time they had moved on he'd be as stiff as a board. Whoever these young ones were they were at home in the woods.

'I ain't going back. I ain't going back.' The boy snuffled. Bream heard sounds that he took to be a tarp being hammered into place.

'You sure as hell took your time!' Kentish snarled at Old Joe, who had been scouting around for signs of Bream. For some inexplicable reason the sight of the old Indian tracker now infuriated him. Half the hunting party had been downed and the old man ought to have had more care. He ought to have warned them before they followed him up that goddamn trail. When this was over they would hang Joe. He deserved to dance at the end of a rope. And to hell with Floyd! But Kentish did not believe that Floyd would be that perturbed about Joe's fate. He could always get himself another tracker.

'I'll take first watch,' Joe volunteered. 'We ride at dawn. We find Eb Bream pretty damn quick!' Joe watched as the men set to and made camp. Jake, from the saloon into which Joe had never dared venture, took it upon himself to make stew while one of Kentish's men, whose name Joe did not know, made bread of a sort. The talk around the fire was of Bream and what they would do to him once they got hold of him. Then a waddy raised the prospect of Bream's launching a surprise night attack against the camp.

'Bream long gone, long gone,' Joe volunteered.

'Just hush your damn mouth. I ain't speaking to

you,' the man, Williams, growled.

'It ain't likely,' Kentish rejoined. 'Williams, you can watch with Joe.'

Williams cussed loudly. 'If I catch you snoozing, Joe, you ain't going to wake up,' he growled threateningly, 'cause I'm gonna stomp you good!'

Kentish laughed unpleasantly. 'None of that kind of talk, Williams. Old Joe here is gonna lead us to Bream. Ain't that so, Joe?'

Joe nodded. Sooner or later these varmints intended to turn on him. But he had plans of his own. 'Got a cigar boss?' he asked Floyd Peters.

'You gotta earn it.' Floyd deliberately lit himself a cigar. 'You get us Eb Bream and I'll give you a whole damn boxful.' Needless to say Joe would not be getting the reward money Kentish had offered for Bream. A box of cigars was good enough for Joe.

'Sure thing, boss,' Joe rejoined.

'Good dog,' someone said. And they all laughed.

After eating, as darkness fell they turned in. Joe bided his time.

'Where the hell are you going?' Williams demanded truculently when Joe stood up.

'I gotta squat,' Joe replied bluntly.

'Don't even think of sneaking off,' Williams growled. 'You take too long and I am gonna start hollering. Savvy?'

'Sure thing,' Joe rejoined. Williams was a dead man. Joe's heart sang with joy that Williams was the one ordered to share the watch.

Williams sat with his back to the darkness, studying the embers of the dying fire. Maybe he could get one of Bream's ears as a souvenir. He could thread a length of rawhide through the ear and wear it around his neck. He smiled. And he died, happily contemplating this act of savagery.

As usual, Tony Kentish was the first to wake. His bones ached. He felt cold. And then memories came flooding back. His beloved Travis was dead, gunned down by Bream, the town bum. He felt so sick with grief he could hardly move, but the feeling passed as the need for vengeance took over. In an instant he was on his feet, shouting for the camp to rise. They had business to attend to.

Men, half-asleep still, came to their feet, belching and scratching and complaining, but the still-blanket-covered form by the dead fire did not stir. It had to be Williams, for the form was too rounded to be the scrawny Joe.

'Goddamnit Williams, get up,' Kentish shouted, greatly incensed for Williams had fallen asleep whilst guarding the camp and the second shift had not been awakened to take over. For good measure he booted the slumbering man. It was then he found out that things were very wrong. The form felt hard, flesh did not yield beneath his boot. Kentish jerked back the blanket. It was when he turned Williams over they all saw that Williams's throat had been slit from ear to ear. 'What the hell!' Kentish cried as he reeled back. 'Bream! He's hit the camp. He's done for Williams and Indian Joe.'

'Hell, he could have killed us all!' Gregory Bagshot exclaimed in great excitement.

71

Floyd scowled at the Bagshot boy. The fool had plenty to learn. And so did the rest of them. He wondered how long it would take for them to figure it out. There was no way Bream could have sneaked up on Old Joe. Those goddamn varmints, Kentish included, had pushed the old Indian a mite too far. Joe had quit. And slit Williams's throat with the greatest of pleasure.

'Well, I reckon I ought to have given him that box of cigars.' Floyd attempted to make light of the situation.

'What the hell do you mean!'

'Well, it's obvious, ain't it! Joe's upped and quit. He did not take kindly to being called a mangy dog or threatened with a kicking.'

'You went along with it,' Jake accused. He spat.

'What the hell! I reckon we can manage well enough without him.'

'I say let's go after him. Williams was my pard. He never deserved this!' a waddy yelled angrily.

There were loud murmurs of agreement and cries that Joe was gonna be strung up and left to rot.

Kentish stepped in. 'I'll blast the first man of you that goes after Joe. We're here to run down that varmint Bream. We get him first. Do you hear me! And only then do we go after Joe.'

Floyd shook his head. 'No. I've got better things to do than look for Joe. One manhunt suits me just fine, I ain't embarking on another one. And if Williams let an old galoot three times his age get the better of him, well, it does not say much for Williams!'

'I can track,' Pedro volunteered. 'I can track good.'

'You've got yourself a job then, son,' Kentish rejoined magnanimously. 'You get me Eb Bream. And I'll do right by you.'

'Yes sir.' Pedro could hardly wait to start. He had blotted out how Eb Bream had snuck up on him and got the upper hand.

At long last Bream had managed to doze. Fortunately he did not snore. A loud howl interrupted his snooze and he came back to reality pretty damn quick.

'You know the dangers,' a woman's voice screamed. She sounded old. There was the sound of a slap and then another howl. 'Stop snivelling. Do you hear,' she screamed, 'I can't abide snivellers. Now you young ones get back home before I really set to and wallop the both of you. You know it ain't safe out here. You know the traps have been set. If the bogey men don't get you very likely the traps will! Get on home, do you hear?'

'I ain't going,' the girl screamed.

'Well, looks like I've gotta drag you by the hair then.' There were the sounds of a scuffle and the girl screamed out for Grandma to let go of her hair. 'I'm gonna drag you home. It's for your own good. You young ones ain't never to sneak off alone.'

Bream listened as the sounds diminished. Even then he did not venture from his hiding-place immediately but lay still, ears strained for the slightest sound. It came sooner than expected and that sound was a goddamn scream, distant but audible. He stayed put. He had a hunch one of his pursuers had blundered into one of the traps the old woman had been talking about. He envisaged metal teeth biting through bone and found himself hoping Kentish was the one who had been snared. Kentish or that polecat Jake.

Pedro had been unable to pick up Bream's trail. The trees pressed in from either side but there was a trail of sorts that led upwards. Pedro figured Bream would have taken the trail. He wished he had not volunteered to track the potman. He was now lead man and the others followed hard on his heels, Kentish breathing down his neck. 'You ain't gonna let me down boy!' he had said more than once in a tone Pedro did not much care for.

'No sir, Mr Kentish, you can rely on me,' Pedro replied a mite too quickly, as he dismounted and made a great show of studying the twisting trail ahead. The horses seemed skittish and not so manageable. Pedro led his horse. Indeed, he concentrated more on the horse than he did on the trail beneath his feet. Behind him the others cussed Eb Bream.

'We've got him!' Pedro pointed at the hat triumphantly. The hat was dirty and battered and looked mighty like the hat Bream wore around town. The old hat was all the confirmation he needed that he was on the right trail.

'Why the hell didn't he pick his hat up?' Butters, one of Kentish's men, pondered aloud. 'Eb Bream ain't no fool, although he let folk think he was!'

'How the hell do we know?' Jake snapped angrily. 'The bum is running scared. He ain't bothered about

74

a hat. There ain't much sun hereabouts.' He looked up as he spoke. The trees blotting out the light made the forest a gloomy sort of place. Jake would be glad when they were out of it. 'We'll ask him when we get him. Is that good enough for you, Butters?'

'I was only asking!' Butters griped.

'Get on!' Kentish shoved Pedro. 'Stop gawking at that goddamn hat!'

'Yes sir, Mr Kentish.' Pedro speeded up as best he could. The leaves underfoot were thicker now, deadening the sound of their progress.

'I reckon . . .' Butters had been about to say he did not reckon the hat had belonged to Bream after all, for he'd noted a bedraggled feather stuck in the hat band, and Eb Bream had never worn a feather in his hat, but before he could finish his sentence a steel trap triggered by Pedro's foot, sprang shut with a vicious twang.

Pedro screamed with pain and kept right on screaming in agony. The steel teeth bit into his flesh, easily penetrating his old boot. His leg was aflame with the pain of it. He went crazy with pain.

'Get it open!' Butters was the first to find his wits. 'Come on. Lend a hand!' Kentish was just standing there glaring at Pedro.

'Well, Bream ain't responsible for this.' Floyd Peters drew his Peacemaker and glanced around anxiously. 'And if he ain't who the hell is?' His voice was drowned by the howls from Pedro. Peters like Kentish was totally uninterested in Pedro's plight. Fact was, Pedro was now a liability. And old Joe would never have put his leg in a bear trap.

'Done it!' Butters and Gates, perspiring with effort, had managed to force open the mouth of the trap. Robinson, one of Floyd's men, quickly removed Pedro's mangled ankle. The trap jaws sprang shut once more, this time biting empty air instead of flesh, as Butter, cussing loudly, hurtled it to one side.

'Goddamnit, that trap ought to have done for Bream,' Kentish snarled. 'How the hell did he avoid it if he headed this way?' He glared accusingly at Pedro, who was now rolling on the ground and clutching his leg as he continued to howl, well beyond speech.

'Forget about Bream!' Floyd yelled. 'We need to know who set that goddamn trap and, more importantly, where are they.' He paused. 'We don't know nothing. And until we know why I guess the safest thing is shoot first and ask the questions afterwards. Agreed!'

'Agreed!' the men chorused.

'I reckon we oughta turn back,' a lone voice argued. 'Maybe old Joe knew something we don't.'

'I'll kill any man who tries to quit now,' Kentish yelled. 'We stick together. There's safety in numbers. And as for Pedro, we can't tote him along and sure as hell we can't leave him suffering!'

'I'll do it!' Guy Bagshot hauled out his shooter.

Pedro, mad with pain, half-crazed still, retained enough of his senses to know what was intended. Cursing in Spanish, he grabbed for his shooter and shot Guy Bagshot fair and square in the chest.

'You've killed my goddamn brother.' Gregory put a shot into Pedro's head.

76

'We're cursed,' Butters declared. 'Joe knew it and that was why he quit!'

'Another word out of you, Butters, and I'll kill you myself,' Kentish yelled. 'We're gonna do what we came here to do. We're gonna get Eb Bream and if anyone gets in our way we're gonna blast 'em.' He ignored the downed Guy Bagshot, who was clearly dead.

Bream heard the shots. He stayed put. Whoever these folks up here were they were gonna clash head on with that damn hunting party.

Gregory Bagshot knelt beside his brother, cradling Guy in his arms; they had always fought like cat and dog but now Guy was gone, blasted by that no-account varmint Pedro, one hell of an empty space had been left. And not one of the men he was riding with seemed concerned by Guy's death!

'I'll take the lead,' Kentish declared, knowing darn well that no one else would. 'If we get hold of whoever set this trap we'll settle with them,' he declared. He eyed Gregory Bagshot who was clearly no damn use now. 'Get your grieving done, then follow on.'

'I aim to bury my brother!' Gregory was ready to blast Kentish should the rancher disagree.

'Quite right,' Kentish agreed. 'Catch up when you can, Gregory.'

Gregory remained alone, crouched beside his brother. How the hell was he going to explain Guy's death to their pa? He'd had enough. He would bury his brother and go home. Fact was, he was damn scared.

'Howdy there, stranger.' The voice was soft. Gregory came to his feet reaching for his shooter until he saw that the simple-looking *hombre* approaching up the trail had a child with him, a girl, clean enough in faded dungarees and thick plaid shirt, small feet shod in moccasins, freckled face pale and unsmiling.

'Why howdy,' Gregory replied. 'Say mister, do you know who the hell set this goddamn trap? Was it you?'

'No.' The round, simple face beamed, revealing a mouth missing a great many teeth. 'Not me.'

'Who the hell . . .' Gregory began but he never got to finish his sentence, for the girl rushed forward and sank her teeth into his leg.

'What the hell!' Gregory doubled over as he reached down intending to grab the little varmint and prise her away. He never saw the blow that killed him, never saw the grinning woodsman heft the hammer that descended with a thud and caved in his skull.

'Grandma will be pleased,' the child thrilled.

'Yep,' her uncle replied. 'Yep, I reckon she will.' He grinned foolishly. 'More food for the pigs, more food for the pigs, and that's a fact.' He scratched his head. 'What the hell has brought 'em up here? Well, they won't be heading back down, no way!'

CHAPTER SIX

He heard them coming, and he was able to recognize some of the voices. By this time, he was so damn stiff and cold he could scarcely move. He knew he was a sitting duck if they found his hiding-place. Gut instinct told him to stay put. He held his breath as they passed within feet of his hiding-place. They were blaming him for whatever had happened on the trail. He heard snatches of conversation, which were enough to tell him that concealed steel traps had been set. Whoever had set those traps would know by now that they had company upon the way, he reflected. Maybe things would work out to his advantage, for other players had been introduced into this lethal game of hunt and kill.

Miz Jenny had been unable to eat or sleep properly since Eb's departure. She'd plastered on her powder and paint and made out she didn't care but it was a damn lie. When Vernon forked it into town she was out on the sidewalks with the rest of them eager for news.

'Well, we ain't seen no sign of Bream,' Vernon rejoined as townsfolk yelled out demanding to know what was going on. 'Bad luck has been dogging us, and we have had one hell of an accident on the trail. Men are down and hurt real bad. Get the wagons! And fetch Doc! He's needed urgent.'

Miz Jenny was almost overwhelmed with relief. She sauntered closer to Vernon, hoping she appeared disinterested, yet wanting to learn more. Vernon to her great astonishment was now gabbling on about Bessie Bliss, and how Eb Bream had blasted Willard. And how Musgrave was going to take care of things.

'What the hell are you talking about?' she yelled. 'Bessie and me are good friends.'

'Go see for yourself!' Vernon turned away. He saw the wagons were coming, and Doc was with them.

Miz Jenny headed back into the saloon. She possessed a riding-habit that had seen better days. There was nothing for it, she must ride out and see whether Bessie needed help. It then suddenly occurred to her that Preacher Child, who had already returned to town, must have known all along about Bessie and Willard, and that damn polecat had not said a word. 'Get the preacher,' she hollered. 'He's needed. There are mortally injured men out there. Get the preacher!' She knew damn well Child would not wish to sit on a horse again. Unused to time in the saddle, Child had been hobbling when he had returned to town. Well, a little more discomfort was what he deserved. She was pleased to see her words take effect. Men were going in search of the preacher. He would not be able to avoid his duty.

*

Old Indian Joe appeared at the kitchen door. Musgrave had not heard his approach.

'What do you want?' Musgrave asked bluntly, wondering how it was the hunting party had let Joe go. Instinct warned Musgrave not to ask! Trusting his instinct had often saved his life. He trusted it now.

'I want a job. I want a place to stay.'

Musgrave considered. The man was too old to be on the move. 'I reckon you've found one! I need help, for I've hurt my back hauling Miz Bliss. I'll pay a fair wage. Just do what you can. And keep your eyes peeled. We don't know who might ride by! You might have to make yourself scarce if you spot someone you don't want to run into.'

Joe nodded. He knew Musgrave referred to Kentish and Peters. Musgrave was a wise man, Joe reflected. His words had saved his life, for Joe had decided to kill the man if insults were offered.

'Frank Musgrave, I'm hungry,' a woman's voice yelled.

'No you ain't, Bessie. You must wait till supper.'

'You're starving me!'

'I ain't, Bessie.' Musgrave grimaced. It was true he had hurt his back. 'Maybe you can cook up the chicken soup, Joe!' he suggested. 'She's gotta start losing weight, so it's got to be rationed. That varmint Willard sure was loco. Hell, all she wants to do is eat.'

'Sure thing.' Joe grinned as he headed towards the barn. He guessed Kentish and the rest of them had met up with the murderously inclined Crockets. Joe had known about them for years. Anyone who ventured into Crocket territory was liable to end up as hog food. He could have told them had they been willing to listen. This place suited him. He aimed to stay.

'What a goddamn stench,' Jake exclaimed. He pulled his bandanna up to cover his nostrils.

'Hogs!' Butters volunteered. 'My pa raised 'em!' The sloping upward path had emerged into a clearing. Trees had been felled to make it. 'There's one of 'em!' Butters pointed at the quarter-grown hog rooting amongst the tree-stumps.

Kentish drew his Peacemaker.

'Well, these trees ain't been felled recently,' Floyd observed. There was something about this set-up that did not set right. He likewise drew his shooter.

'Well, I'll be damned,' Jake pointed. An old woman had appeared at the far end of the clearing. She hobbled towards them. When she smiled toothless gums were revealed.

'Welcome, strangers. We don't often see strangers these parts,' she cackled.

'We!' Kentish instantly challenged.

'Just me and my kin. We live hereabouts. Why, you are welcome to join us for a meal and home-brewed liquor.'

'You wouldn't know anything about a mantrap set back on the trail?' Floyd questioned.

She rubbed her hands together. 'We've a rogue grizzly hereabouts. He's been sneaking around. I couldn't risk it getting one of the young 'uns. I'm heartily sorry if the trap took one of your men. But we don't get strangers in these parts, leastways not often!'

'Then you ain't seen a lone man on foot?' Kentish essayed. 'Have you seen anyone?' He glared at her, ready to pounce if he thought she lied.

Seemingly unperturbed by the implied threat, she squinted knowingly at Kentish. 'It's like that, is it? You're seeking retribution. Well, we ain't seen him but my kin can help you track him down. Tomorrow my boys will get the dogs out. They'll flush him out if he's hereabouts. Naturally we'd expect a small token of goodwill for the use of the dogs.'

'He's hereabouts,' Kentish stated with certainty.

'Why do you want him?'

'I aim to roast him real slow,' Kentish snarled, unable to put into words that he had lost his son.

She cackled, 'Like I said, tomorrow my boys will unleash the dogs and flush him out. Least we can do, seeing as how we harmed one of yours.' Being no fool she knew what drove this hard-eyed man. She turned away. 'You just follow me. We've got boiled pork, fried pork, prime chops, why, I even make my own sausages.' Without waiting for their reply she shuffled away, pretty damn sure they would follow her. The ploy worked without fail every time.

'I don't like it,' Kentish hissed. 'Keep your eyes peeled and at the first sign of trouble we'll blast these varmints. We'll do it anyway once we get Bream.'

'Leastways we'd be able to look Ronnie in the eye,' Butters muttered. 'These loons have done for his boy.' There were mutters of agreement. 'There must be womenfolk,' Butters continued, licking his lips.

'Hell, Butters, you may not be particular but I am!' Floyd jested. He paused. 'Like Tony says, we'll see to matters after we've got Bream. The truth is without old Joe we need these folk to run him down. Pedro was no damn use and that was a fact.'

'What do you mean by see to matters?' a waddy asked.

'Hell, just use your imagination,' Jake rejoined with a suggestive wink.

As soon as dawn broke Bream left his hiding-place. Late last night there had been the brief sounds of gunfire. But not enough of it to suggest that the whole damn hunting party had been blasted. 'Damn shame,' he had muttered. 'Damn shame!' But something had gone on up ahead. He stretched his aching bones. Rain was beginning to fall. Maybe that would be enough to deter whoever might give pursuit. With Kentish and the hunting party ahead he intended heading back down because he assumed Kentish was going to be detained by whomever he had run into. There'd been men on the trail before dusk had fallen, cussing each other and toting supplies judging by the snatches of conversation he had overheard. It was his intention to return to the Bliss place in the hope that he would find Miz Jenny there tending Bessie. Gut instinct told him that Kentish and the hunting party would not be returning from these hills. Whoever was up there clearly did not want it known.

*

'This town bum has led you a merry dance,' the old woman cackled.

Kentish bit back an epithet, while a few of the men suppressed a laugh. They had been shown into the eating-house, an oblong of a hut the inside of which was dominated by a long table. Women waited silently on the men as they and the old woman ate. And not one of the women was young and attractive, Kentish had noticed, thereby determining that those who were had been kept purposely out of sight.

'My boys can eat separate tonight,' Ma Crocket had told them. 'You're my guests. There ain't nothing too good for you. It ain't often I see strangers. My boys go into Potters Creek from time to time. Just for supplies. They don't linger.' She cackled again. 'Town bum or not, he has led you a merry dance,' she reiterated.

'He's been lucky, ma'am,' Kentish replied, forcing himself to be civil. Her hunting dogs had impressed him. He had conceded he needed those dogs. 'So why are you living out here, ma'am?'

She didn't even have to think. 'Why, to keep my kin away from the wickedness of the world.'

'The hell you say! Beg pardon, ma'am,' Jake exclaimed.

'So how do you like my pork and taters?' she enquired.

'Just fine, ma'am,' Floyd Peters rejoined.

'Help yourself from the jug. It's my own brew. Can't touch it myself. My innards ain't got the strength to deal with it. It's mighty potent.' She cackled again and grinned widely. 'Now drink up.

85

Tomorrow we'll get Eb Bream. My dogs will run him down. They've been trained specially for the task, although of course their natural prey is bears. Mighty tasty they are too. And the fur comes in mighty useful.' Glenda Crocket stuck a plug of chewing-tobacco into her mouth. Her gums moved. The damn fools were drinking. She had known they would. They were fair guzzling her home brew. 'It ain't like it's strong liquor,' she reassured them. 'Ain't no one going to get drunk at my table, never fear!'

Outside, her three sons, grandsons and one great grandson waited. Near by, out of sight the smaller kids of the clan waited, trained not to make a sound for fear of a walloping. Pretty soon the men inside the eating-house would be clutching their bellies, rolling around howling they'd been poisoned, help-less when the men rushed in. The 'guests' were a valuable commodity, providing clothes, shooters, ammo, horses, money and hog food. Life was hard hidden away in the woods.

Butters keeled over first. Clutching his belly, he yelled out he had been poisoned. One by one the others followed suit while the old woman chomped her baccy, watching them with small bright birdlike eyes.

'You've done poisoned us.' Robinson clutched his belly with one hand and reached for his shooter with the other, but the old woman had already left the table and was scooting for the door. Robinson fired at her anyway, but pain caused him to shoot wide before he collapsed.

Floyd Peters drew his shooter. He knew what was coming. They'd been led into a trap. Tony Kentish likewise got his weapon out. As the men rushed through the doors Peters and Kentish fired wildly before they collapsed.

Glenda Crocket howled like a crazy woman as she saw two of her boys go down before her 'guests' were clubbed senseless. Only then did the Crocket men look to their wounded kin. For they had been trained well by Glenda. Bertram, Glenda's firstborn was dead, whilst Abraham had escaped with a shoulder wound.

Glenda Crocket began to howl and swear vengeance on the two men, Peters and Kentish. There'd be no merciful release before those two went into the boiling-pot, she yelled. They'd go in alive. And they would be the last to be boiled. And the fact was she now aimed to boil the whole darn lot of them alive. Them who were waiting their turns could watch the others suffer.

And as for the man Bream, she was not surprised they had not bagged him. Years back, she had fallen out with one Clara Bream. They had fought on Main Street and Clara had won. It did not matter that Clara had been dead for many years. Glenda remembered her humiliation as though it had been yesterday. Tomorrow they would hunt down the man who could well be Clara's grandson. She would have her revenge at long last. He too could go into the boiling-pot. But for now she must only think about Abraham. There was a bullet to remove. Glenda prided herself on her medical skill. She always scrubbed her hands well with carbolic and wounds were cleansed with strong whiskey – why, she was as good as any so called doc. And as for Bertram, well she would grieve only when she was sure Abraham was going to make it.

Whatever it was the old varmint had given them had worked swiftly and powerfully. The agonizing stomach cramps had hit without warning. Nor did they ease when light began to creep in through the one barred window of the building in which they were imprisoned. Not that any one of them could reach the window! When they had come round they all found themselves securely chained at the ankle. Iron rings had been set into the floor. This building was clearly a prison, a squalid, miserable pen fit only for pigs; one of them was actually rooting around in the straw as a gap-toothed youngster grinned at them through the open doorway.

'We're gonna get out of here!' Floyd Peters croaked. Realization hit him. Old Joe had known this tribe of half-witted loons were holed up in these woods. Old Joe had known and let them ride into a trap. Well, he would deal with Joe by and by.

Kentish retched but was unable to fetch anything up. He'd vomited it all up during the night, as had they all.

'Goddamnit Kentish, you're gonna be the death of us!' Robinson accused.

Tony Kentish could scarcely believe one of his men would dare address him in such an insolent way.

'You're fired!' He didn't realize how ridiculous the words sounded.

'And you're mad, Kentish. Do you think that old

devil is gonna let us ride out of here.' Robinson paused: he had nothing to lose now. 'Travis had it coming, for he was a mean-hearted varmint who took pleasure in picking on those weaker than himself. This time he picked on a better man. He got his just deserts. Fact is, we were all scared to speak the truth. Well, now we're all paying the price for turning against Eb Bream, a man who just wanted to be let be!'

'You shut your lying mouth!' Kentish would have attacked Robinson had he been able.

'I ain't lying. They all know that!'

'Shut the hell up, both of you,' Peters yelled. 'We're gonna put our minds to getting out of here. And when we get out we're heading back to town. The Army can deal with this bunch of crazies and Eb Bream can go to the devil. As far as I am concerned he ain't important.'

'Bream—' Kentish began.

'Ah, to hell with Bream!' Jake exclaimed. 'I should have known that beanpole was nothing but trouble as soon as I saw him. If the crazies don't get him he can go to hell. But I ain't going with him.'

The door of the prison creaked open and a man of middling years hobbled in. He grinned at the prisoners, revealing a mouth of rotted yellow teeth. Behind him was a boy of about thirteen toting a .45.

'Keep back, you varmints,' the older man snarled, setting down the two buckets of water he was toting. Hobbling, he went out and returned with tin mugs which he put down near the water.

'What the hell do you aim to do with us?' Peters exclaimed.

'Your kind comes in handy for hog food.'

'Our kind. What the hell do you mean?'

'Outsiders. Ma can't stand outsiders.' He paused. 'We rely on the hogs for most things, food and leather, come winter we butcher most of 'em. But we always have hogs in need of victuals. Like Ma says, you outsiders come in useful.' He cackled, 'But it ain't your turn yet away, we've got three dead 'uns from the trail.'

'The Bagshot boys and Pedro!' a waddy exclaimed.

'Well, I can't say what they were called but that sounds right.'

'What's your ma doing now?' Peters asked with mounting horror.

'Why, she's tending Abraham and then, when the rain stops, we aim to bury Bertram.'

'It ain't raining,' Kentish could see the open doorway.

'But it's gonna. And badly. So it looks like Eb Bream is in luck! The dogs can't track him when it's thundering and lightning. Seems like the devil is taking care of him for now. Ma sure is disappointed, for she once knew a Clara Bream, wife of Kingdom Bream. Now there was a man, Ma says.' He shook his head and then, grinning lopsidedly, he ambled out.

Along the way Bream picked up the doll. The rain was falling in large, heavy drops. It was dark beneath the trees and he spotted the doll solely because he was keeping his eyes peeled for traps, moving slowly, feeling his way with a fallen branch. He did not know what prompted him to pick it up and put it in his pocket.

*

Rosie Hobbs ambled into Brindissi's hotel. For some reason the man's wife was always glad to see her, although why the woman was glad that Angello Brindissi had been brought home safely Rosie found hard to fathom. Mrs Brindissi's gratitude was expressed by insisting that Rosie did not pay for her meals. She was a guest, an honoured guest, Mrs Brindissi said.

Well, sure as hell Rosie kinda liked being an honoured guest. Sitting alone she poured herself a cup of tea.

Brindissi poped his head round the door. 'Good afternoon, Miz Rosie.'

'Good afternoon, Angello,' she replied primly. Things were looking good. Miz Maud nagged plenty, although Miz Maud did not see it that way; the crew weren't up to much; Juan was too old and Ned slow-witted, but Rosie aimed to stay put. The worst of it was they were all expected to attend church service every Sunday along with Miz Maud; that was hard to stomach but . . .

'Miz Rosie.' Howie burst into the restaurant.

'What is it?'

'It's Ned. Two galoots have plied him with liquor and have got him down on his knees braying like a mule. He thinks it's fun, poor fool, but I reckon things are gonna turn real bad. They look kinda mean. Can you get him out of there, real pronto?'

Rosie stood up. 'Save the table. I'll be back.' She sighed, was it too much to expect Ned to stay out of trouble?

'Ned ain't to blame, Miz Rosie.' Howie ran along behind her. 'He knows he ain't allowed but one drink and he told 'em, but they kept on filling his glass, and making him drink up.'

The two hardcases lounged against the bar. On the floor the huge dimwit was now, at their insistence, barking like a dog.

'Leave him be, You can see he ain't right in the head,' the bartender urged.

'Ned!' one of the saloon women yelled, 'you get out of here. Do you hear. You ain't allowed more than one drink. You know that. When Miz Maud hears of this you'll be in big trouble. Your new foreman's gonna tell her for sure.'

Ned stopped barking. 'It ain't allowed,' he slurred. 'I'm gonna be in big trouble when foreman finds out, big trouble.' Ned began to blub.

'Well, you ain't finished here yet awhile. I've a mind to hear you be a chicken. Start squawking.'

'It ain't allowed,' Ned blubbed. 'I'm in big trouble. Yes sir.'

'You're arguing with me, are you? Well I don't take kindly to being argued with.' The voice was soft but the man's eyes were feral. 'I guess I'm gonna have to cut you down to size.'

'Now hold on—' the bartender began.

'You've got a death wish, have you, barkeep!'

'No sir,' the bartender saw to his shame that his hands were shaking. Ned was in mortal danger and there was not a damn thing anyone could do.

The batwings swung open with a vengeance.

'Get out of here, Ned. Go stick your head in the

horse-trough.' Rosie Hobbs surveyed the scene in disgust. 'I know you ain't to blame!'

'Yes, Miz Rosie,' the man cried.

'Not for too long mind. I don't want you drowning.'

'Yes, Miz Rosie.'

'What the hell!' one of the hardcases exclaimed as Ned, lowering his head and hunching his shoulders, rushed out through the batwings. They did not attempt to stop him but stared at the woman, who in her choice of clothes and the fact that she wore two guns was nothing like a woman was supposed to be. And then they began to hoot with laughter and let rip with a string of epithets.

Snider spat. 'You old hag. You done spoilt our fun.'

'Yep,' she agreed. 'And now I'm gonna kill the both of you. Pretty damn quick. My tea is getting cold.'

Snider hooted with laughter, unable to believe what he was hearing. His companion suddenly noticed that no one else in the saloon was laughing. Indeed, men were moving away out of the line of fire and all the saloon women had already ducked down behind the bar.

'I'm counting to ten. Best make your move because at ten I'm hauling iron,' Rosie Hobbs observed calmly. Slowly she began to count.

Snider reached at eight, with his pard reaching a second later. As they reached she reached and she was faster, her heavy weapon leaving its holster with practised ease. Rosie downed them both, one shot through the belly, he was the unlucky one, the other through the heart. She holstered her smoking gun, the gunsmoke leaving an acid smell in the air. All around, shocked faces looked at her and then looked away, as if afraid to catch her eye.

'They got their just deserts,' she stated calmly. She eyed the bartender. 'I'll excuse you this time as you served Ned under duress, but remember, he ain't to have more than the one drink. It's for his own good.' She holstered her guns. 'Now I've damn well got to load the supplies myself as Ned in his present state can't be trusted not to go dropping things.'

'I'll do it, Miz Rosie,' Howie cried, 'You can't be hefting heavy sacks, why it ain't no job for a lady.'

'Shame on you, Howie. Why I do believe you're angling to become better acquainted with Miz Rosie,' a saloon girl cried. 'Miz Rosie, you had better start running, for Howie is after you.'

'Now then, Molly we'll have none of that kind of talk! I am a respectable woman.'

'I know you are, Miz Rosie,' Howie cried. 'And I am a gentleman, I can assure you.'

Samuel Pilgrim, sitting at a corner table, almost choked on his beer. He had unconcernedly watched Snider and the Texan bait the idiot. He had made no move to stop the show because Samuel Pilgrim did not give a damn about anyone save his twin sister Veronica. Pilgrim had recognized her immediately, Rosie Hobbs the female gunslinger who until now had worked the border areas. Maybe Snider had not recognized her because rumour had it Hobbs was pleasing to the eye. Rumour was untrue. She was fast,

Pilgrim conceded. As fast as himself, but Pilgrim was not interested in finding out who was best. He killed solely for money.

Slowly he left the saloon, Jakes Place it was called. Outside on Main Street Ned was still dipping his head into the horse-trough.

'That will do, Ned,' Hobbs bellowed. 'Get yourself to the livery barn and wait there.'

'Yes Miz Rosie.' Ned was off at the double.

Howie, Pilgrim noted in disbelief, had actually taken Miss Rosie's arm and was escorting her down Main Street.

'The world has gone mad,' Pilgrim muttered. She had seen him, of course. She had recognized him. Knowing that he killed solely for profit and not for reputation she had chosen to ignore his presence. He guessed she would ask around to discover what had brought him to the town of Kentish.

Pilgrim directed his footsteps towards the livery barn. It was time to move out. His disappeared sister and her no-account husband Hubert Smith had not passed through this town. It sure was puzzling, Veronica and her no-account husband had disappeared from their dugout just south of Potters Creek. They had been gone some time. Pilgrim had found the place deserted, cleaned out, dust-covered and no one in Potters Creek seemed to know a damn thing about it. Pilgrim was now sweeping the territory hereabouts, painstakingly looking for clues.

All the folk in this town had wanted to talk about was an *hombre* called Eb Bream. There had been an accident on the trail during the pursuit of Bream. A good many men had forked it out of town in order to bring injured posse members back to town. And bets were now being taken as to whether one Tony Kentish was likely to make it back safely.

Pilgrim saddled his horse. He did not give a damn about any of them. He had to find Veronica. He could not rest easy until he knew she was safe and well.

CHAPTER SEVEN

Hubert Smith had not cared much for Pilgrim and had accused him of being a mindless killer. 'But for the sake of your sister I can tolerate you once in a while,' Hubert had magnanimously declared.

Pilgrim, after a sizeable absence, had intended to pay one of his once-in-a-while visits. But he'd drawn a blank. The homestead had been deserted, and for some time too!

In Potter's Creek he had also drawn a blank. The storekeeper had told him the Smiths had been doing just fine, but had not been able to recollect the last time they had bought supplies. And other folk he had questioned had replied: why, they did not recollect the last time they had seen the Smiths. Which was mighty odd considering Hubert had put great store in churchgoing. There was something odd about that town, he had decided. But whatever it was, folk were not saying. He guessed he must root it out and if that meant lighting a fire beneath someone's foot so be it. But first he wanted to scout around and pick up on any rumours that might be circulating. It was a long shot but he had been hoping the Smiths had upped and moved to the nearest town. And that just happened to be this one, hence his presence in Jake's Place.

His sister's home had been cleaned out: table, chairs, bedding, pots, pans – all were gone. Dust coated the floor. But his sister would have left word in town for him if necessity had forced them to up and leave. Pilgrim had lit his pipe. Maybe the sour-faced store-keeper's wife had destroyed the missive. Sure as hell he would get round to questioning the pair. He had disliked them on sight, for they had looked down their long noses at him, but he had not allowed himself to take umbrage over a look!

Pilgrim was not a family man. Howling youngsters set his teeth on edge. He could not abide them. Why, even his two young nieces were hard to stomach. They howled and whined at the drop of a hat. Their pa, Hubert, was a sanctimonious bore and his sister talked too much about Hubert and the girls, but the thought of anyone harming them had thrown Pilgrim into a murderous rage which he had great trouble in concealing.

As he rode out of the town, he reflected that perhaps he had been too soft on the Potter's Creek folk. He ought to have put his pistol to the head of the storekeeper's wife and told her what she was going to do. 'You'll tell me,' he should have said, 'what became of my sister Veronica Smith and her no-account husband, not forgetting those two girls or else, my dear, why you'll be minus your head, for I don't give a damn what becomes of you. And if I have erred why it'll be too darn late to rectify matters.' And not one of those no-account bums in that town would lift a hand to stop him riding out. Pilgrim appreciated the power of fear, and how it paralysed no-account bums.

He had one last place to check out. That was the spread owned by the late Willard Bliss, dispatched, apparently, by hunted fugitive Eb Bream. There was something mighty odd about that place but, whatever it was, folk were not saying. But he would find out for himself soon enough. A man called Musgrave was now in charge, so Pilgrim had heard.

Chickens scattered at his approach, and a small dog dashed out from beneath the porch, thought better of barking and retreated, growling softly. Pilgrim thinned his lips, just the kind of welcome he had come to expect. Dismounting, he ignored the old Indian who sat on the porch swathed in a heavy blanket, eyes fixed on the horizon as his rocker creaked back and forth. Clearly loco, Pilgrim decided! It came with age, if one lived long enough. His kind seldom did.

A woman stepped out on to the porch, a hard-eyed woman with wide swinging hips and strong arms, he noticed with approval. Sure as hell, with her powdered face and painted lips she did not belong out here. Standing her ground she regarded him with suspicion and dislike.

'Where's Musgrave?' he asked without preamble.

'Out and about attending to chores!' Her voice was sharp.

'I'm looking for my kin. They go by the handle of Smith. Veronica and Hubert and two young ones. Girls. Have you seen them or heard of them?'

'Nope.'

The rocking-chair creaked. Pilgrim did not turn round. 'I reckon they might have called in here on their way to the town of Kentish.'

'Willard is dead so he ain't saying. But I can ask Miz Bliss if you like.'

'And you are?' he enquired.

'I'm Miz Jenny.' She raised her voice. 'Bessie, have you seen strangers, a couple and two girls?'

'No,' came the cry from inside the house.

Miz Jenny shrugged unconcernedly. 'Don't let me keep you, stranger.'

'Pilgrim.' He introduced himself with pride. 'Samuel Pilgrim.'

'The gunman!' she nodded. A movement behind the front door brought him instantly alert and ready to haul iron.

'No need to trouble yourself. It's just Miz Bliss,' she reassured him. 'We're alone here.'

'Apart from your hired man!'

'Hired man!' She frowned. 'Oh, you mean Joe. Well he's more part of the family now. He helps out when he can, when he has a mind,' she clarified.

'Part of the family!' Pilgrim essayed. Was she losing her mind!

'Well, me and Miz Bliss kinda rely on him. He can rustle up some mighty fine meals when he has a mind.'

To Pilgrim's disbelief a huge woman waddled out

100

on to the porch.

'I done washed the dishes,' she whined. 'Tell Joe to cook.'

'Now Bessie,' Miz Jenny chided, 'you know damn well it ain't time to eat. We have meal times round here. He'll cook when it's time. And you know he ain't going to get moving until he is ready.'

'Jenny, please!'

'Now I ain't running after no chicken, Bessie, and I never learnt to make bread. You've just got to wait. I ain't cooking. It ain't my forte.' She turned her attention to Pilgrim. 'Don't let us keep you. Hospitality ain't our forte.'

Pilgrin bowed. 'I'll bid you two ladies good day.' He winked at Bessie. 'You're damn lucky he don't serve up dog stew.'

'You get off my place,' Miz Bessie screamed as, to his great astonishment, her face grew red. 'I don't care for that kind of talk. Get out of here!'

'I'm leaving, ma'am, lest you topple upon me. I aim to keep breathing. I daren't risk it!' Pilgrim was actually enjoying himself now and was determined upon the last word. And he would have left there and then had not something that the dog had dragged out from beneath the porch caught his eyes. 'Goddamnit!' he yelled as he retrieved it, his fingers closing over the wooden doll. He stared at it intently. It was the one! He had carved it himself, deliberately making the nose extra long and the ears a trifle pointed. His nieces had loved that doll, although his brother-in-law had been unimpressed. Pilgrim lost control. 'Where did you get this doll?' he roared.

'What the hell do you know? A knife appeared in his hand. 'Start talking!'

It was then that an object, hard and stolid, struck Samuel Pilgrim on the head with force sufficient to fell him. He went down with a grunt.

'No, Joe,' Jenny yelled, for Joe clearly intended to slit Samuel Pilgrim's throat. 'Sit on him, Bessie. I'll get the rope.'

'Slit his throat and save yourself one hell heap of trouble,' Joe advised. Nevertheless he allowed himself to be pushed aside by Bessie, who promptly sat upon the luckless Samuel Pilgrim.

'We'll put him out in the barn for now,' Jenny declared. 'We can dispatch him by and by if needs be.' She eyed Joe. 'We'll talk with him by and by. And then decide what to do with him!'

Joe nodded. 'This man is big trouble. You save yourselves big trouble by killing him.'

'We've got to do what's right,' Bessie bleated.

'Well, Miz Bessie, it is right to kill him. You'll see by and by,' Joe rejoined. 'But for now, why I'm gonna catch a chicken and make soup. You hogtie him, Miz Jenny.' And then for all Joe cared Samuel Pilgrim could be left to rot!

Musgrave had always relied upon instincts. They had kept him alive so far. So when Eb Bream had turned up out of his mind and racked with fever, hobbling along, his feet a sorry mess, starving, tormented with thirst and babbling wildly about Miz Jenny, he had declared that Eb was welcome to stay as long as needs be and Miz Jenny was welcome to nurse him back to health. Nothing else could be said because Miz Jenny was looking at him oddly, and at that time she had been holding a kitchen knife in her hand, gripped real tight and about ready to attack anyone who threated to harm Eb.

'I ain't got no quarrel with Eb,' he had hastened to clarify, 'But maybe Miz Bessie won't see things that way, he blasted Willard after all!'

'Bessie has gotten over that varmint Willard. And if you are thinking of proposing to Bessie to get your hands on the ranch then think again. If there is any proposing to be done she will do it herself. Savvy?'

'Well, I have branding to attend to, Miz Jenny. But bear in mind this place needs a man and I am as good as any.' But she had not been listening. Her attention was focused solely on Eb Bream and Joe was actually at the stove brewing up a decoction to help Eb recover. Muttering to himself, Musgrave had ridden out.

As he returned all looked the same as he had left it. A thin spiral of smoke snaked its way skyward. But as he came closer he noted a strange horse in the corral.

Bessie appeared on the porch. And actually smiled to see him. 'Afternoon Frank.' Her voice was high and sounded odd coming from such a huge woman. 'Just in time for chicken soup. Joe is cooking.'

She was looking thinner, he noted, but he sure was tired of chicken soup. 'So how is Eb?'

'Joe reckons he'll make it.'

Musgrave entered the house. He peered into the room where Eb Bream lay. The dog, he saw, had made itself at home at the foot of Bream's bed. A Peacemaker lay upon the bedside table but Bream was delirious still. He wasn't particularly worried about Kentish and the hunting party turning up at the door, Joe having assured them that boss Kentish and the rest of them were done for. Of course Jenny and Bessie had wanted to know what he meant but Joe had ignored their questions and eventually both had grown tired and shut up. Musgrave himself had known not to ask.

'Anything happen whilst I was away?' he asked.

'Oh well, Samuel Pilgrim came by,' Miz Jenny replied casually. 'And threatened us with violence. Joe took care of him. Not that I let Joe kill him, although upon reflection Joe might have had the right idea. The man is a no-account killer, after all!'

'Hell! Where is he?'

'Why, tied up in the barn. Joe is looking out for him,' Miz Jenny replied.

Joe, Musgrave saw, seemed engrossed in the chicken soup.

'Looking out for him?' Musgrave essayed.

'Why, feeding and watering him,' Bessie explained.

Musgrave, muttering a curse, headed for the barn with all possible speed. There was a stench emanating from the place the cause of which became obvious as he crossed the threshold. Hell, Joe had just left him there, hogtied and helpless. Jenny and Bessie had not bothered to check up on the captive.

'Best put him out of his misery!' Joe had followed Musgrave out to the barn.

'I reckon,' Miz Jenny agreed. 'I'm beginning to feel mighty uneasy about this man. Upon reflection I don't want Eb troubled unnecessarily, for he has been to hell and back!'

Joe nodded approvingly. 'You're talking sense, Miz Jenny!'

'No.' Musgrave stepped between Joe and the hogtied Pilgrim. 'It ain't right. I reckon a whole heap of men have died because they went along with something that was not right. Kentish and the rest of them, neighbours, men I have drunk with.'

'Sam Pilgrim is pure poison,' Miz Jenny declared. 'If we don't kill him he'll be gunning for all of us. We've done him wrong as he will see it. He'll want retribution.'

'No, Miz Jenny, you'll have to kill me first. I aim to get him inside and tend him as best I can, for I am a changed man now.'

'Have you gone mad, Frank Musgrave?' Miz Jenny demanded.

'Now Joe, I ain't never given you an order.' Musgrave ignored her foolish questions. 'Let's say I would appreciate it if you did not kill this man.' To his relief Joe nodded.

Eb drifted in and out of consciousness, and Jenny was always there, encouraging him to take a bit more soup. His Jenny. He came awake with a start, calling her name and there she was sitting by his bed.

'You're back with us then, Eb,' she observed, hiding her delight that he had pulled through.

'I would never have done it without you, Miz Jenny,' he croaked.

105

'My pleasure Eb, my pleasure.'

'Miz Jenny,' he continued, taking hold of her hand, 'if you throw in your lot with me I'll love you to my dying day.'

'Which may be sooner than you think,' a voice drawled. Musgrave entered the room smiling sardonically.

Eb tried to grab for his Peacemaker but Miz Jenny kept hold of his hand, yelling out that Musgrave had seen the light. He no longer worked for Kentish and the fact of it was he had his eye on Bessie and the ranch.

'There ain't no harm in that, Miz Jenny.' Musgrave defended himself.

'Well, that's a matter of opinion.'

Musgrave ignored the pesky woman. 'Samuel Pilgrim wants a word with you.' He addressed Eb Bream.

'The gunfighter?' Bream essayed.

'The very same. I found him hogtied in the barn. Miz Jenny could only think about you, Eb. Hell, she forgot all about Pilgrim! And as for Joe, well it was deliberate. He left that man bound and helpless without food and water. Lord, I hate to think what that man could do to someone who truly riled him!'

'Pilgrim ain't one to turn the other cheek,' Eb advised as he struggled to sit up. 'We have one almighty problem now!'

'Hell, Musgrave has found the Lord,' Miz Jenny explained. 'The darn fool has tended to Pilgrim and now the varmint is as fit and well as he ever was and after vengeance, unless I am mistaken!'

Eb nodded. Lord, his neck felt weak. 'That goddamn varmint will be sure to seek retribution!' He paused. 'Well, I will hear what the varmint has to say. After that, very likely I'll have to deal with him myself.' He eyed his Peacemaker. Which was aptly called, he thought: dead men did not make trouble.

When he tried to swing his legs from the bed he found himself hardly able to stand and was forced to grab hold of Jenny's strong arm. He could scarcely walk. *One foot after the other*, he thought. That thought had got him back to Miz Jenny. He'd just known she would be tending Bessie.

Sam Pilgrim had come around to find himself hogtied out in the barn, and there he had been left to roll around in his own filth without food or water. He'd erred. He had thought the woman could pose a threat. It had simply not occurred to him that the old Indian was the greater threat. He'd been too fool to recognize it and would have paid with his life if Musgrave had not returned from seeing to chores. And now he sat in Miz Bessie's parlour, shackled hand and foot, waiting on Eb Bream. When a tall thin beanpole of an *hombre* leaning heavily on that painted floozie, Miz Jenny, entered the sparsely furnished parlour, gut instinct kept him from disrespecting her, for Eb Bream was clearly besotted. Also old Joe had appeared, studiously cleaning his long nails with the tip of his blade. Joe's eyes, Pilgrim saw, remained flat and expressionless. He put Pilgrim in mind of a snake waiting to strike. The man, he saw now, was without fear and without mercy.

'Well, speak your piece,' Miz Jenny ordered before Eb Bream could open his mouth.

'What can I do for you?' Bream enquired mildly.

The mildness did not fool Pilgrim. 'You can tell me how you came by the doll.' Pilgrim gestured at the doll. It was on the mantel now. 'I know that doll, for I carved it myself and gave it to my nieces, now disappeared along with their ma and pa. What do you know about it?'

'Then why the hell didn't you say so from the first?' Miz Jenny interrupted angrily. 'Why threaten me and Bessie? Hell, Pilgrim, you brought your suffering upon yourself and that's a fact. There ain't no one here to blame for what happened to you. Only yourself!'

Pilgrim forced himself to ignore her. He been hogtied, left to wallow in filth and starved and now she was telling him he had himself to blame. He had Joe to blame – and the two women, for they had never bothered to check on Joe.

'So, you old varmint, do you aim to apologize?' Pilgrim demanded as he eyed the old man with fury.

The old man merely ignored him.

'The doll!' Pilgrim snarled. 'What do you know!'

'Well, the fact is,' Bream rejoined, 'I stumbled upon it up in hill country. It was just lying on the trail where it had been dropped.' He paused. 'You might as well know there's a whole parcel of crazy folk holed up thereabouts. Glenda Crocket's clan, I believe. I kinda remember my grandma talking about how she fled to the hills after having despatched her husband in a particularly unpleasant way. I was young myself then.'

'Real crazy folk,' Joe volunteered unexpectedly. 'A real bad place, Crocket men always steal women. And their men!' Joe shrugged. 'They get fed to the hogs, real bad place.'

'Kentish hog food!' Musgrave exclaimed incredulously. 'Men I've ridden with, neighbours!'

'Well I ain't exactly got any sympathy for them seeing as they were hell-bent on seeing me dead,' Eb declared. He eyed Pilgrim. 'Your kin ain't my problem. You're a man who harbours a grudge, I hear.'

'You hear right!'

'Well I guess we must settle things between us as soon as I am able to stand by myself.' Eb smiled drily. 'I ain't having you gunning for Miz Jenny and Joe.'

'I'll wait for you,' Pilgrim rejoined. It was logical it would come to this. Eb Bream was clearly ensnared by Miz Jenny.

'Now that won't do,' Musgrave was determined to speak his piece. 'Why, if those varmints were to come down from the hills and swing in this direction they would land up on Bessie's doorstep. It ain't likely, I know, but it could happen. I ain't scared for myself but I've gotta think of Bessie.'

'What the hell are you saying, Musgrave?' Miz Jenny demanded.

'Why, it's clear enough. Sam Pilgrim here will swear that he will forgo retribution against yourself and Joe and in return Eb will help him find his kin or, if they are beyond help, exact retribution on the Crockets. So you see this matter can be resolved without gunplay! Leastways gunplay between Eb and Sam.'

'You damn interfering varmint, Musgrave.' Miz Jenny guided Eb to a stool. She picked up a plate. 'You've put Eb at risk. I ain't having it.'

Musgrave threw up an arm to protect his head. 'Hell! Miz Jenny,' he yelled as she hurled the plate.

Eb Bream had to be crazy, Pilgrim decided. The man ought to be running instead of smiling foolishly as Miz Jenny ranted and raved at Musgrave.

'It ain't in my mind to go back,' Bream observed when he could get a word in edgeways. 'We're gonna toss a coin. Heads Pilgrim and me shoot it out, tails I'll guide him back and help him out in return for his pledge to forget what happened here. There ain't no other way to decide this matter. Naturally I'm hoping it will be heads, but I will abide by the way it falls.'

'No need for a coin. I accept your offer,' Pilgrim shouted. His kin were more important than exacting revenge on two women and one man. 'And you!' He regarded Musgrave. 'Why are you so anxious to have me alive?'

Musgrave coughed awkwardly. 'Fact is, my pa was a preacher and I might well have followed in his footsteps had he not died of the fever. I headed West to seek my fortune, but never found it working for Kentish. I guess I have been remembering. And I can truly say I have found the Lord!'

An embarrassed silence ensued. Eb Bream looked away and so did Samuel Pilgrim, whilst Joe made a pretence of scratching his head.

'I feel I've been born again,' Musgrave continued, oblivious to the effect his words were having. 'I can see a day coming when the day of the gun is over.'

'Well it ain't yet!' Pilgrim snarled. 'There's a whole lot of killing to be done. Me and Bream here must rescue my kin and wipe out that nest of vipers. I want 'em to know why they're gonna die. I want 'em to know the mistake of taking my sister and her family has cost them dear.'

'I reckon,' Eb agreed sombrely, wishing indeed that Joe had been allowed to dispatch Pilgrim. Eb was now committed to heading back to hill country. And, as Pilgrim had said, there was killing to be done. Although he liked to think of it as extermination: doing what was right making the hill trail safe for men to ride by removing a great evil.

CHAPTER EIGHT

Bream eyed Pilgrim with dislike. 'But,' he continued, 'we must do our damndest to ensure the women and children stay safe.'

Pilgrim shrugged. 'Our objective is to stay alive and rescue my kin. And to stay alive we must deal with the men of the clan. Naturally I won't lower myself to hunt down women and children but I ain't going out of my way to ensure their safety, as you say!'

'Fair enough.' Eb capitulated. 'All I ask is you don't blast everything that moves.'

'Why, you would turn every man in the territory against you!' Miz Jenny declared. 'Don't you be forgetting, Sam Pilgrim, that your sister may be dead, or maybe deranged; either way you're gonna have to raise those two young girls.' She paused. 'It's obvious, ain't it. You're gonna have to put down roots and try and get along with your neighbours. Your gunfighting days over.' She laughed. 'Well, I can see you ain't exactly thought things through. You must rescue the women who want to be rescued. And for that you will need wagons to transport them all back to town.

112

Those that want to leave must be given money to get them to where they want to go. Kentish and Peters can pay,' she paused. 'We'll get Miz Maud on our side. She sure hates Peters. The bank can release some of their cash. Well, it's only right, someone has got to pay and better the dead than the living, I say!'

'If they ain't dead they're gonna be,' Eb observed grimly, 'I ain't leaving either one of those varmints alive to put a bullet in my back.'

Miz Jenny sighed. 'I ought to have slit your throat myself, Sam Pilgrim, for you are nothing but trouble.'

'Now then, Jenny, you can't fault a man for caring about his kin.' Bream rebuked. 'Nor for wanting to rescue them.'

Miz Maud's face grew red. 'I absolutely insist you hold a funeral service.' She glared at William Child, the town pastor. 'Why, Peter Holt has served this town well for years. He's been a member of your congregation and attended service every Sunday, and yet you refuse to officiate!'

'The man is a suicide, Miz Maud!' William Child stood firm. 'It's regrettable but there it is. I must follow my conscience!'

'We cannot blame him for that. He was told he would not walk again.'

'That's no excuse. I must follow my conscience.'

'Well, in that case you had better get over to the saloon and apologize to Eb Bream for encouraging folk in this town to hunt him down like a mad dog,' Howie, who was with Miz Maud, observed maliciously.

'Bream! Here in town!' William Child could scarcely believe that he had heard correctly. And he also recalled words spoken by Tony Kentish before the ill-fated and now missing hunting party had set out: the reward, blood money, call it what you will, was to be paid out regardless, the bank had been instructed and the order had been written down. 'Whether I am alive or dead I want Bream seen to,' Kentish had self-righteously declared. A good many had heard him.

'Well, Peter Holt is to be buried tomorrow,' Miz Maud continued. 'And you will officiate. Miss Rose will escort you to the church.'

'Miss Rose!' For a moment he did not understand her. Good Lord, she meant Hobbs, that deranged woman who had slaughtered two men at the saloon, that creature who strode around wearing male attire and he too terrified to utter a word of censure less her rage be directed at him.

'The town will pay its respects to Peter. I am determined upon it. Good day to you, Reverend Child.'

Trembling with rage he stared after her. He did not dare berate her for her presumption. Fear of Hobbs kept him silent. The thought sprang into his head unbidden that whilst Hobbs might take umbrage if Miz Maud were thwarted she was highly unlikely to give a damn about the fate of Eb Bream. And it was Bream, after all, who was indirectly responsible for the misfortunes that had befallen this town. Good men were dead because of him. The hunting party would not be coming back He knew it! And, doubtless, Bream was responsible.

114

The pastor hesitated. Wasn't it time he left this town? And the reward money was there to be collected! He stood indecisively on the sidewalk, observing the town, noticing it seemed busier today. Men were drifting towards Brindissi's hotel. As Child stood dithering he spotted a familiar face; indeed, with his mass of red, curly hair and freckled face young Vernon was hard to miss.

'Vernon!' Vernon swung round as Child's hand closed over his arm. 'Thank the Lord you are here,' Child continued solemnly. 'He has given you a chance, Vernon, a chance to make sure your ma wants for nothing. Eb Bream is in town. And the reward stands whether Mr Kentish is here or not. All you have to do is collect it.' And he would make damn sure Vernon did not see a cent of that reward. Child was married to the banker's sister, after all. And surely it would be Child, having set Vernon on Bream, who would have earned the reward. Child had once seen Vernon fooling around, shooting to impress some of the town kids and to Child's eye Vernon looked fast enough on the draw to take Bream.

Vernon swallowed. 'I ain't never shot it out face to face,' he admitted. 'Although that don't mean I ain't able to,' he clarified quickly lest his words be misinterpreted.

'Well, you know what your boss would want you to do,' Child urged. 'And poor Peter Holt forced to take his own life, and Mathew Archer killed outright, mangled beneath the weight of his horse, Willard Bliss brutally gunned down.'

'Well, Willard had it coming after what he did to Bessie,' Vernon observed. 'My ma says so.'

'Maybe so,' Child knew better than to say a word against Vernon's ma. 'And how is she? Arthritis is a terrible curse; what a difference that extra stake would make. You've got right on your side, Vernon. Why, I'll be out here praying for you.' He paused. 'If anyone in this town has the ability, why, it is you. I have faith in you, Vernon. Make your boss Mr Peters proud!' Child waited a moment, then played his trump card. 'You wouldn't want folk hereabouts to think you were yellow!'

Vernon scratched his head, painfully aware that he had been backed into a corner and could not see a way out. If he didn't go after Bream, Floyd, when he heard about it, most likely would sack Vernon. And who hereabouts would want to hire a man labelled yellow? Besides which, Vernon knew he was pretty good when it came to hauling iron. It was just that he had never faced up to anyone. All he'd ever done was fool around to impress a few kids. He swallowed. If he had extra money he would pay a woman to care for his ma.

'I'll do it!'

'Good man!' Child slapped him on the back. By the time Vernon realized he would not see a cent of the reward money Child planned to be long gone.

Across Main Street Rose Hobbs, who had watched the encounter, reached a decision. She was smart enough to realize what the pastor was about. He was going after the money. Not directly but through the use of a dupe. She could have stopped it herself but

116

was wise enough not to belittle Vernon before the eyes of the town. Hell, she did not much care whether Bream was blasted but she had heard plenty about that varmint William Child. She disliked him. And a remark he had made had reached her ears. He had observed quite loudly that Howie needed spectacles. She'd known at once what he had meant!

She hesitated. She guessed that, like herself, Vernon had been raised in a certain way. His life depended on her guessing right. If she was wrong then he was done for. Bream would have to kill him.

Bream had decided to show up in the saloon and thereby give anyone who wanted to take a pot-shot at him a chance to make a move. His reception, however, was warm. Patrons of the saloon had observed that they were glad he was just fine and if anyone was loco that *hombre* was Tony Kentish, who ought to have known that Travis was crazed and was going to get done for sooner or later.

'Why, thank you kindly.' Bream had managed a smile. He knew damn well how to play this game: being diplomatic, Miz Jenny had called it; in other words, smiling when you wanted to spit.

He had relaxed, but not totally. As far as he could see no one in town aimed to come gunning for him. Although there were always those who might shoot from cover, backshooters, but as Pilgrim had pointed out, this town was running scared; anyone who missed first time round was as good as dead and they knew it. 'Because if you don't get 'em I will,' Pilgrim had promised. 'I've put the word out. Anyone who steps out of line has got me to deal with.'

Across Main Street Pilgrim, who was lounging against a post, had also observed what was afoot. That varmint of a preacher was sending the young fool Vernon after Bream. Pilgrim remained untroubled. Bream would blast Vernon; a lesson, if it were needed, for anyone else who harboured such thoughts. Idly he wondered why Rosie Hobbs was rushing off. Her behaviour was erratic, but then he forgot about her when he saw what Child was about. To his astonishment, the pastor was now kneeling and praying loudly. A small crowd had naturally gathered.

Ignoring the lunatic, Pilgrim headed for the saloon. The atmosphere inside vibrated with tension, for Vernon had already confronted Bream, and to Pilgrim's astonishment Bream was trying to reason with the idiot.

'Now you must know Travis Kentish was a no-account bum,' he was saying, tone reasonable. 'Everyone else in town knew it so why not you?'

'I ain't here to palaver,' Vernon yelled. 'I'm waiting on you, Eb Bream, to make your move.'

'What if I don't!'

'Well I'm gonna reach anyhow, so I reckon you ain't got no say in the matter.'

'Well, I reckon not,' Eb agreed softly, thinking that regrettably he had no choice but to kill the young fool. Lord, would no one in this saloon speak up and try to dissuade the man, if one could call him that, from this foolishness which was destined to end in death. 'Death ain't a pretty sight.' Eb tried one more time, aware that Pilgrim, who had entered the saloon, was grinning hugely. The varmint was enjoying this.

'I'm counting to ten then I'm reaching,' Vernon stated defiantly. But he got no further than three.

Lizzie Smith, Vernon's ma, burst through the batwings, the first time ever she had entered a saloon, closely followed by Rose Hobbs. 'Stop,' she cried, positioning herself between Vernon and Eb Bream, both of whom were staring, unable to believe this turn of events. Pilgrim put two and two together faster than the rest of them. Hobbs was responsible for this. She had gone and fetched the boy's ma. He couldn't believe it!

'I won't let you kill my boy,' Mrs Smith cried wildly.

'No, ma'am,' Eb muttered uncomfortably. He recognized the look in her eyes. Crazed was how Grandpa Bream would have described it. 'Someone put him up to it anyhow,' he muttered.

'Now, Ma,' Vernon began. 'You get on out of here.'

'We don't take blood money,' his ma yelled. 'We're respectable folk.'

'Forget it, Vernon,' Bream urged. 'No one will think the worse of you. A good man don't argue with his ma, especially when she's in the right. Ain't that so, Samuel?' He glared at Pilgrim. 'Ain't that so?'

'It's the gospel truth,' Pilgrim rejoined with a smirk. 'And I'll blast any man who says different.' He winked at Bream. 'Preacher Child oughta have known better!'

Lizzie grabbed her son's gun arm. 'You ain't doing it. You ain't hauling iron.' She hung on desperately.

'No, Ma,' Vernon agreed. No one laughed. Fact was most men looked kind of embarrassed.

'Elizabeth Smith, this is men's business. There's no need for you to worry yourself. Vernon is top-notch. I can vouch for him.' William Child stepped through the batwings unaware that he had erred. 'A respectable woman has no place in this place. Shame on you, Elizabeth Smith, for entering this place of sin.'

'It's true. What Miss Rose said is true,' Lizzie cried wildly. 'You've gone mad, Preacher Child.' Her left hand gripped Vernon's gun arm, her fingers digging into him through the fabric of his shirt as she desperately tightened her grip. Her right hand reached for Vernon's .45. It was heavy, cumbersome even, but she found the strength. 'No,' she yelled as she shoved Vernon away with a scream; for one heart-stopping moment Bream thought she was going to blast him. He'd frozen, unable to haul iron and blast the deranged woman even to save his life.

Pilgrim likewise had frozen. Shooting down a woman would set the whole town against him. And what Miz Jenny said was truth. He might have to make a home for himself and the girls. For the first time in his life he needed good will.

The shot reverberated in the saloon; the smell of gunfire hung acid in the earth. Clutching his stomach Child fell to the floor.

'No, Ma,' Vernon cried, knowing they would hang her for sure. William Child was not yet dead but he was on the way.

'Well, it seems to me he was about to reach for the derringer he carried,' Rose Hobbs observed. 'Seems to me he was about to shoot Mrs Elizabeth Smith. If anyone says different, we'll have a word!'

No one spoke. Every man in the saloon remembered how Hobbs had just recently killed two men in this very saloon.

'Self-defence, no doubt about it,' Eb croaked. He wiped his brow. 'Better take your ma home.' He addressed Vernon. 'She'll need a pot of tea,' he added, remembering how his grandma had sworn by tea.

'Plenty of it,' Hobbs advised.

'Come on, ma.' Vernon took her arm as he removed the smoking gun and holstered it. He'd been frozen himself, powerless to stop her, because for a moment there she'd seemed actually demented. 'Tea,' he muttered. 'That's what you need. And a lie down.' He himself wanted a slug of whiskey but did not dare suggest it.

'Well, someone best get Doc,' Eb observed.

'No point, he's done for,' Hobbs observed. She frowned. 'Hell, who is gonna officiate at Holt's funeral?'

'Well, that ain't a problem. Musgrave's pa used to be a preacher. I reckon Musgrave can recall the words. He'll do it with pleasure,' Eb declared.

'Well, I'll ride on out and bring him back to town. We've gotta have that funeral or Miz Maud will be right put out,' she rejoined.

'What the hell got into you,' Pilgrim hissed. 'That woman, that Lizzie Smith could have shot you.'

Bream shrugged. 'Sure as hell I don't know. I guess I just couldn't blast the poor creature. At least some good has come out of this. Young Vernon is gonna steer clear of gun play. Hell, Pilgrim, had he bested me it might have gone to his head. He could have been on the way to ending up like you.'

'Child ain't got no derringer. He's too damn yellow to carry one,' a waddy declared.

'If Miz Rose says he was toting a derringer then he was toting a derringer,' the barman butted in. 'There ain't no one in this town going to argue with her except maybe Howie and he's sweet on her. And sure as hell he don't care about Preacher Child.'

'Get him out of here,' Pilgrim advised. 'Before he starts attracting flies.' *Hombres* intent on getting a drink had in fact stepped over the prone form of Child in order to reach the bar.

Bream watched as the dead man was toted out. No one seemed to care. That was folk for you, he reflected drily, thinking that if Rose Hobbs had cared enough to save Vernon, there must be good in the woman buried deep in there, nevertheless.

'Well, he wasn't much of a man,' a saloon girl observed. 'I've seen his wife sporting a black eye more than once. I kinda felt sorry for her.'

'Damn fool,' another woman declared. 'Her kind would not spit on one of us if we were on fire.' She shrugged. 'Well, I reckon Mrs Child will have cause for celebration – not that she dare let on.'

Bream, heading for the hotel with Pilgrim at his heels, agreed with the sentiment. Not that he would voice such feelings.

Brindissi, bestowing a smile of welcome, showed Eb into the back room where ranchers and senior towns-men were gathered. Eb winked at the hotel-keeper.

'You joined that goddamn hunting party, didn't you?'

'Si,' Brindissi wondered whether Bream would blast him. 'A moment of madness,' he clarified.

Bream shrugged. 'Speaking of madness,' he addressed the assembled company, 'I'm here to tell you about the Crockets.' Without preamble he related what he knew about Glenda Crocket and her kin. 'So it's clear,' he concluded, 'that they are taking whoever they can, probably keeping the women and kids and feeding the men to the hogs.'

'Do you reckon that's what has happened to Kentish and Peters?' a man asked.

'I reckon so,' Eb replied. 'They ain't back, are they? But they ain't our concern. Sam Pilgrim and me aim to mount a rescue party of two to find and rescue Sam's kin and any other unfortunate souls we find there. And who better to provide the needed funds than Kentish and Peters. We aim to ask the bank to release the funds from their accounts to help the women and children we rescue. Miz Maud and Miz Rose agree that it's gotta be done. And we believe that Kentish and Peters would pay out willingly if they were alive. And if they are dead it does not signify!'

Floyd Peters refused to give up hope. He was a good-looking man as far as the ladies were concerned, with the exception of that cantankerous viper Miz Maud, so now he had set about making some kind of impression on Eden Crocket's daughter, a stout and unattractive female whom Eden toted along to help out when he tended to the prisoners. It wasn't easy but Floyd pegged away at it, slipping in a compliment

123

here and there, thanking her kindly whenever he could and making out that he was interested.

'One of us has got to get out and fetch help,' he reminded the others. 'And I believe Sue is kindly disposed towards me.'

'You don't stand a chance,' Tony Kentish rasped.

'That Sue Crocket ain't quite all right,' Jake had observed. 'So maybe you do stand a chance, for she appears to have taken a shine to you.'

'Well, I'm making my move,' Floyd declared. 'I aim to propose to Sue. If she aims to be Mrs Floyd Peters she's gonna have to make her move.' He shook his head. 'It can only be the one of us. Hell, we can't all ride out of here. The timing has gotta be right.' He knew damn well what was going to happen. Sue had found the opportunity to whisper in his ear. He also knew damn well what Glenda was planning: a celebration for the recovery of her son Abraham.

Susan Crocket was in love and with one of the outsiders as well. She was going to be Mrs Floyd Peters if only she could get him out of here. Sue Crocket walked around with her head in the clouds. No one thought anything of it, for it was understood that Sue took after her Pa Eden in that she was none too bright. Sue's ma had died early and it had been Eden who had hauled Sue up, feeding her when he remembered and cursing her when she disturbed him.

Well, now she had someone, a handsome rich man who was going to take her away and make her his wife. Nor was she a fool. She knew exactly what had to be done to get them out of here. And she knew when it was to be done.

CHAPTER NINE

'You should have searched for the varmint.' Abraham Crocket took a mouthful of his ma's chicken soup. 'He's a danger to us.'

'I thought you was done for,' his ma croaked. 'With infection setting in and all.' She shook her head. 'I don't reckon he'll be coming back. Besides which we've done him a favour. We've taken care of the galoots on his trail.' She spooned another mouthful of soup into her eldest. 'I sure would have liked to get my hands on Clara Bream's grandson. I hate that woman. She bested me out on Main Street. I can remember it all as though it were yesterday. I never did get my revenge.'

'Now Clara has been dead for years,' Abraham observed as he had done many times in the past. 'And you know it ain't possible to take revenge on the dead.'

'It sure as hell is. She'd be looking down, watching over her grandson,' Glenda rebuked.

Abraham grunted: this conversation was going nowhere. 'So you've got entertainment planned, have you, Ma?'

'Well, I reckon we need cheering up! It's about time those varmints started to sweat a little. They need a taste of what is in store. Things didn't go as planned with this particular bunch and Bertram has been planted because of them. We're gonna celebrate your recovery this very afternoon. Ain't no point in delaying!'

'They're roasting one of the hogs this afternoon,' Susan Crocket told Floyd. She grinned, revealing a set of rotten teeth. 'We'll be leaving this afternoon. We gotta! Now don't you fret none. I got it sorted.'

Beneath the dirt that covered his face Floyd paled. He knew she meant there would be hog-roasting and something else besides. Hogs were slaughtered and dried just before winter fell. Other times they were only killed and roasted for a special event. If Sue Crocket had spoken plainly the imprisoned men would have gone berserk. Floyd wondered which one of them had run out of luck! If staying alive in this hell hole could be called luck.

'It ain't right you get to go and we get to stay,' one of the men growled angrily at Floyd once Sue Crocket had shuffled away.

'If one of us don't get out none of us stands a chance,' Floyd rejoined patiently. 'I'll be back with help. We'll blast the whole darn bunch of them. Besides which, she ain't stupid enough to release the whole darn bunch of us. I've taken her fancy and that's a fact, so I guess I am the lucky one, if one can call having to smooch with Sue Crocket luck! I want to puke every time I see her.'

Tony Kentish thinned his lips. By the time Floyd got back the whole darn bunch of them could be dead for all he knew. Floyd would be back because if even one of them survived and made it known that Floyd had not returned with help Floyd would be finished in the territory. Floyd knew it. They all knew it. Floyd was a forlorn hope but the only hope they had. 'You come on back, Floyd, do you hear? Round up all the men in the territory. You smoke these varmints out and burn the lot of them!'

'You can count on it,' Floyd promised.

Eden Crocket had chosen Butters because he was the fattest of the bunch. Also Butters was fast going crazy and Eden reckoned the crazy ones were the hardest to manage. 'You're gonna be the guest of honour,' he told him with a leer. At which Butters, near mad by now, began to sob.

'Hell, Butters, be a man!' Kentish exclaimed.

'You shut your goddamn mouth, Kentish,' one of the men yelled angrily. 'Or Lord help me, you are done for. I'll kill you myself.'

'Don't do it,' Eden advised. 'Ma wants him saved till last. You make Ma angry, son, and Lord help you. The Devil sure as hell won't, for he favours Ma.'

Glenda Crocket worked the women like slaves getting the victuals prepared and the great trestle tables set up. When it was done Susan Crocket slunk off and left them to it. She headed for the shack she shared with her Pa. Eden lay on his bed, drunk. Susan removed the key for Floyd's shackles, and stood for a while as she pondered possibilities. Then she hefted Eden up, placing her shoulder under his arm, and guided him out towards the great table.

'Put him here alongside me,' Glenda ordered.

'Yes, Grandma.' Susan dumped Eden on to his chair. His head fell forward.

'Throw a bucket of water over him so he don't miss the proceedings,' Glenda ordered.

'Sure thing,' a grandson cried.

Susan slunk away. Women didn't count for much in the Crocket clan unless there was hard work to be done. The men sat at the top of the table with Glenda, the women and kids down at the end. 'I ain't feeling well. Reckon I'm gonna throw up,' Susan muttered as she passed by the other women.

'Best get out of here,' one advised kindly. 'Sure as hell Glenda will come down on you hard if you interrupt the proceedings.'

'Enjoy the fun,' Susan muttered. Butters she saw was already being dragged towards the top of the table. He would take pride of place tied to a chair placed between Abraham and Glenda. He had not quite worked out what was going to happen. His realization and terror was all part of the fun!

Floyd Peters had never been so glad to see a woman in his life as he had Susan Crocket. He'd always doubted she'd go through with it. But he'd kept his doubts to himself.

'He ain't going 'less we all go,' Jake declared. 'You free him and we'll set up such a commotion those no account varmints will have to hear.' And they would, no matter that the no account varmints were making one hell of a din themselves. 'We're all agreed,

Floyd,' he continued. 'It's not we don't trust you but we'd be fools to miss our chance.'

'Floyd's key is different,' Susan Crocket rejoined. 'One of these will do for you lot.' She placed a bunch of keys down just out of reach. 'One of you galoots will be able to reach them. Meanwhile me and Floyd will be leaving. Come on, Floyd.' Taking his arm she steered him towards the door.

There was no one about, the huge table being set up some distance from the far side of the hut. 'Hell, they ain't going to make it. They'll give the game away,' Floyd observed but Susan Crocket was already guiding him through the gate of the stockade, and to Floyd's relief there was no sign of any guard. 'Them ain't the keys' she grinned. 'By the time they work it out we'll be long gone. There ain't no one gonna hear them yelling once the fun begins.'

The settlement was surrounded by a high, pointed-log fence. On both sides were watch-towers which Floyd understood were always manned.

'I've taken care of things,' Sue smirked. 'I'm Crocket through and through and you had best remember it, Mr Peters,' she concluded with a simper that revealed stained teeth.

Floyd kissed her hand. They were large hands toughened by toil. 'I will always be grateful to you, Susan. You have saved my life. How could any man not love the woman who has risked herself to save him?' He was not expecting an answer but to his surprise she obliged.

'I didn't really risk myself. Those two boys were easy enough to dispatch.'

'What are you saying?'

'Just that I had to get rid of them. The towers are never left unmanned.'

'What?'

'Just whacked each of them over the head with a hammer. It had to be done if I'm gonna be a lady and be Mrs Floyd Peters. Now come on. You follow me. We're heading out on the river. There ain't no one gonna catch us, Floyd. As soon as we hit civilization you can make an honest woman of me. There won't be no hanky-panky till then if you know what I mean.'

'I sure do. And there sure won't.' Floyd panted as he followed her into the woods. He had no choice but to follow, for he was lost without her.

'I know these woods like I know my own hand,' she assured him.

Floyd knew he smelt like a polecat after his sojourn in the Crocket barn but Sue Crocket had never noticed for she stank herself. They all did. None of them set store by washing. Now Miz Maud, whom he surely detested, always smelt of lavender soap. First thing he was gonna do was pay Miz Maud a visit. It was high time he exerted his authority. She had to realize she was not gonna get out of the wedding. He'd fire those useless bastards she employed. The old Mexican and the simpleton had to go. He'd replace them with his own men. Miz Maud would not find one friend in town. The whole darn bunch were chicken!

They were moving downwards now, heading towards the river, he guessed. The path was narrow but well-trodden.

'I love you, Susan,' he told her. She deserved to feel happy.

'Oh Floyd,' she simpered. 'And I love you too. We're gonna be together for always.'

'You ain't never gonna look at another man Susan.' And that was a fact.

'Oh Floyd,' she simpered. 'I never would.'

'I believe you.' They had reached the river now and he noted with approval that she had holed all the boats but one. And in that one boat was victuals, his rifle and his gunbelt, instantly recognizable for he'd had it emblazoned with red stars, and there, in its holster, was his Peacemaker.

'I've just got to kiss you, Susan,' he cried. 'Just the once. Close your eyes and pucker up.'

'Oh Floyd!' Dutifully she closed her eyes.

Well, she had earned a kiss, he decided. She'd sprung him from that hell-hole so he'd pay his due no matter what. With a grimace Floyd kissed Susan fair and square upon the mouth and then, before she could open her eyes, before she had even an inkling of his intention, he snapped her neck. And then let her fall to the ground. It would not have been so easy had she had an inkling of what was coming but he had taken her by surprise.

He stepped into the boat and cast off. He put Susan Crocket out of his mind. His thoughts turned to Miz Maud. That uppity woman was going to learn humility! Things were not turning out badly. It had always been his aim to expand and Tony Kentish's ranch, with Tony gone, would be up for grabs. Add

131

that to Miz Maud's modest spread and he would be well on his way to becoming a cattle baron.

Jake's long arm felt as though it were coming out of its socket, as he bellied down and reached for the set of keys. They were just out of reach. He could touch them with the tips of his fingers but not draw them close.

'The bitch!' he grunted. 'She's done it deliberate. She's deliberately placed them out of reach. She ain't as stupid as she looks!'

'You get away from those keys,' a voice shrilled. Lally Crocket stood in the doorway, horror written over her face. 'You varmint!' She snatched up a pitchfork and headed towards Jake.

'No, miss, I ain't gonna move, I swear it,' Jake yelled. And that was true for he lay stretched out flat on the floor, his leg tethered at the ankle by a short length of chain fixed to a loop set into the wall.

Still holding the pitchfork Lally Crocket rushed forward and bent to retrieve the keys. Jake, without regard for anything, grabbed for the woman's ankle and tugged, bringing her down with a scream which he promptly stifled by placing a hand over her mouth. Lally Crocket, wriggling desperately, let go of the keys and bit ferociously into the hand over her mouth.

Jake cursed and before he realized what he was doing did what came natural, he started to strangle the woman whilst Tony Kentish, ignoring what was taking place, grabbed for the keys.

'Got them,' he yelled triumphantly, leaving Jake

clearly out of his head to get on with the task of dealing with the struggling woman, a woman who could not be allowed to raise the alarm.

'Find the key, goddamn it,' voices urged.

Outside the feast had concluded. Glenda Crocket had always enjoyed a hanging. Most folks did, the sight of a man or woman dangling on the end of a noose being considered good entertainment. There'd already been entertainment of sorts already, for Glenda had spotted Lally at the far end of the table. Seizing a baked tater Glenda had hurled it at Lally. She'd missed, the distance was too great for her, but Lally, having a bad temper, seized up a tater and hurtled it at the old woman. And Lally had not missed. Roars of rage from the clan had followed and Lally had fled. Glenda was shaken. Goddamnit, she was getting so old that even being hit with a tater was gonna leave a bruise. The young had no respect! She turned her attention to the one they called Butters. She must act as though being hit with a tater had not shaken her. Any sign of weakness and she would lose her authority.

'You're the star turn,' she croaked. The children were drawing cards to see who was going to be the lucky one chosen to pull on Butter's legs as he drew his last breath. 'Fetch him,' she ordered. 'Let's go see the hanging-tree.' A roar of approval greeted her words. And when he was dead he would go into the pot along with the rest of the leavings, the whole lot would be boiled up into a kinda mash for the hogs. The kids, she noted, were skipping with glee, even the two new ones, young girls snatched from an

133

outlying homestead. Well, they were Crockets now and that was a fact. They'd do. Those who did not adapt were gotten rid of pretty damn quick.

The girls kept dancing. They'd always been quick learners and had not forgotten a game taught them by their uncle. It was called playing at being good, he'd explained. And then their pa had yelled out that being good was natural and did not need to be played at. Deception, their pa had yelled, that's what you're teaching them, Samuel Pilgrim. And then Ma had come with the cake and the argument was over. They knew now not to ask when Ma and Pa were coming back for it only got them yelled out.

'None of them goddamn keys fits,' Tony Kentish yelled. 'She's played us for fools. None of them fits.'

A waddy grabbing the keys from his hands desperately tried to find one that suited.

'Goddamnit, Jake. We ain't covering for you. You killed that woman and you're gonna have to admit it!' Robinson yelled at Jake, desperation written over his face.

'To hell with you,' Jake snarled. He retrieved the pitchfork that they had used to retrieve the keys and balanced it experimentally. 'The first one of them in here is gonna get their just deserts. We're done for in any event.'

Outside Butters began to scream for mercy.

'Eden, you take two of the boys and haul Kentish out here. I want him to see this,' Glenda yelled. 'I want him to see my cooking-pot and the fire. I want him to know what's coming.' She stood up. 'Fact is, I'll come along myself. You shut your squalling,' she turned on Butters, 'or you'll go into my pot breathing. You would have done anyway 'cept the young 'uns wanted their fun.'

Butters clamped his lips together. He was not so far gone as not to know the evil old crone was in earnest.

Sweat poured down Jake's brow. Clumsily he had clambered to his feet. He readied the pitchfork. He was done for in any event so he might as well go down fighting. Goddamn it, what a fool he had been, wanting to curry favour with Tony Kentish. And he ought never to have taken pity, as he saw it, on the goddamn bum, Bream. He ought never to have given him a job. He balanced the pitchfork. He would have but the one throw and he must make it good.

Glenda had decided that the disrespectful Lally must be made to eat a bar of soap. That would learn her! But for now those varmints in the shed were gonna learn what it meant to wander into Crocket territory. The door was ajar she saw, and that was wrong for it was to be kept shut and barred at all times.

'Eden!'

'What, Ma!'

'The goddamn door. You jest can't be trusted, can you! You no-good skunk.'

'It wasn't me,' Eden whined, sure he was not to blame although he could not recall whether he had shut and barred the door or not.

'Get out of my way, you skunk!' She shoved him to one side and entered first.

As the old woman came through the door Jake hurled his pitchfork. Though weakened from confinement he nevertheless dredged up the strength and the pitchfork sailed straight and true right into Glenda Crocket's scrawny chest.

Eden Crocket stood as if turned to stone as his ma crumbled. And then he uttered a howl the like of which had never been heard before as he launched himself at the man who had killed his ma, scarcely noticing poor dead Lally as he did so.

Crockets poured into the barn drawn like flies to dead meat. To the relief of the prisoners, who had the good sense to cower away from Jake, the fury that had been unleashed now was all directed at Jake. They knew he was a goner. That was for sure, but everyone of them was glad that it was Jake and not themselves. No one was so foolish as to lift a hand to try and help the doomed saloonkeeper.

CHAPTER TEN

Sue Crocket, the Lord bless her, had packed victuals.
Floyd, who had beached the boat to take a breather,
wolfed down a pie without stopping to consider what
he was doing. Realization hit him. Goddamn it, the
pie was pork, and they all knew what those goddamn
hogs got to eat from time to time. To settle his stomach he took a gulp of tepid beer. And then chewed
on a hunk of soft bread. He was out of it. He had
made it. Now all he had to do was get back to town
and send one of his men to the nearest army post. No
one in their right mind would go up into the hills to
take on the Crockets but the army did not have a
choice. Of course, by the time they got there Kentish
and the rest of them might have been butchered but
Floyd found he did not very much care.

Idly he speculated whether the Crockets used
deceased kin as hog-food. Maybe not as the dead
one, Bertram, had, according to Eden, been buried
right and proper. But would these rules apply to a
traitor to her kin such as Susan Crocket. He got back
into his boat. He had a hunch this river flowed even-

tually somewhere near enough to Potters Creek for him to make it on foot to town and there get himself a horse. Sue Crocket had muttered something to the effect that they must be sure to watch out for the shack because it would be time to leave the river.

By now, of course, Miz Maud would think herself safe. She would be certain he would not be coming back. Well, he aimed to teach her different! It was about time she learnt he was not a man to be crossed. He needed a woman real bad and Miz Maud was gonna be that woman. And he would boot those two useless critters she called her ranch hands out pretty damn quick. Maybe he'd blast the pair of them should they be unwise enough to argue with Floyd Peters.

Rosie Hobbs was feeling mighty pleased and all because of Ned. He'd heard something she had not and Ned did not know when to keep his mouth shut. He'd taken to following her around, bleating: 'Is it true Miz Rosie? Is Howie gonna propose?'

'Well, I am sure I do not know, Ned,' she had told him a hundred times.

'But you must know, Miz Rosie, because he's gonna propose to you,' Ned had endearingly replied a hundred times. Well, there was only one fly in the jam, so to speak, and that fly was Mr Floyd Peters. She'd have to blast him if he ever came back, that was for sure. The man was a goddamn troublemaker! He was fuelled by avarice. He saw himself as a cattle baron. There was only one way to deal with his kind!

*

Floyd Peters beached his boat. There was the shack, set some way back from the river, a thin ribbon of smoke leaving the chimney, evidence that someone was at home. Floyd decided it was best not to go on straight up to the front door of this place, not until he knew what he was getting into. After what he had been through nothing was ever gonna surprise him again. Floyd accordingly disappeared into the scrub that grew alongside the river. And just in time, for three figures came out of the shack.

'What the hell?' Tully scratched his bald head. 'One of the Crockets was here, that's for sure.'

The women were Crockets born, Floyd decided, for the Crocket women born into the clan, not the taken ones, tended to favour round faces and snub noses. These ones, bulging out of their tawdry gowns, were undoubtedly Crockets and if they took after Susan Crocket they would be found to be none too bright. The man was another matter, for he was tall and scrawny with the look of a cadaver about him. He sported a stubble chin and deep-set eyes.

Esmeralda Crocket scratched vigorously. 'We've got company coming.'

Tully looked round. Whoever had come down by river was keeping out of sight not unusual, he thought, for lone Crockets tended to slink around, believing there was more safety in numbers.

Tilly Crocket picked her ear. 'Two of 'em,' she grunted.

'Well, gentlemen, have you come for pleasure?' Tully greeted the two men from town with a wide smile.

139

Tully saw himself as a middle man, a go-between if you like. Glenda Crocket needed to buy supplies and for that she needed money. On her behalf he bought the supplies and the two Crocket women sent down by Glenda, by bestowing their favours, earned money to buy those supplies. Tully took a modest cut. He also directed the Crockets to newcomers to the district, those who could be safely raided and snatched.

Tully, after pocketing the money, sat himself down upon a log whilst the four disappeared into the shack. Tully stared at the river, not so fast-flowing now, having spent itself in its descent from the hills. The shack was built on higher ground just in case of flooding.

Some galoots would stoop to anything, Floyd decided. He himself would not have touched either of those Crockets with a bargepole. Time was getting on. He needed to get moving lest those varmints gave pursuit. How long were they gonna be inside that damn shack? Well, Susan Crocket had thoughtfully provided a sharp blade. Old stovepipe hat, whoever he might be, was a goner.

Tully continued to stare at the river. Whoever had come down would be out by and by, once the two men had gone. The women needed changing, Tully decided, for men liked to see different faces. For a big man Floyd moved silently, a large hand clamped over Tully's mouth as the blade sank deep between Tully's shoulder-blades. The four inside never stood a chance in hell as Floyd Peters kicked in the door and blasted away, oblivious to the squeals and cries for mercy. In fact he felt darn good afterwards!

Floyd did not trouble himself searching for money. All he wanted from here was a horse. Thanks to Sue Crocket he had water and victuals aplenty. Floyd mounted the horse which he was glad to see had been well tended. Old stovepipe hat had presumably been prepared for a quick getaway on a sound animal.

His conscience was clear. Crockets were scum and so was anyone who associated with them. Why, anyone who countenanced what these Crockets got up to deserved to be blasted and that included varmints visiting this shack in pursuit of pleasure. Whistling cheerfully, Floyd headed not to Potters Creek, the nearest town, but back to his town, the town of Kentish. Eb Bream was forgotten. The whole darn bunch of them was forgotten. All he could think about was uppity Miz Maud and making her pay. She ought to have jumped at the chance of accepting his proposal.

Tony Kentish and the men huddled together in fetid darkness. Robinson was fast losing his mind. And they all believed they were done for. Jake had been beaten to pulp and Butters had gone into that huge pot, shouting and screaming and kicking and begging for mercy. They had all been forced to watch and listen until the end. And now they had been left to sweat until things had settled down.

There was discord amongst the Crockets now that the old woman who had ruled them for so long was dead. Two of the grandsons had been so bold as to voice the opinion that maybe it was time for the clan to come down from the hills and live like normal folk.

Abraham Crocket, who thought himself leader of the clan now, had vociferously pointed out that this was hardly possible. Everyone in Potters Creek, save the newcomers knew what went on up here. If they were to leave the safety of hill country it would not be long before folk tried to hunt them down like mad dogs.

'Let 'em get a sniff of weakness and they will be on us,' Abraham had declared. His authority was shaky; he had wanted to put Susan who had killed two of her own and betrayed them all, into the pot but he had been shouted down. And so Susan had been buried with the rest of the kin. There was fear in the settlement because never before had such misfortune befallen the clan. Abraham's decision was that they should dismantle the settlement and move deeper into hill country. All they needed was a suitable site. They would cover their tracks and lie low whilst they waited to see what happened next. But some in the settlement were so cowed they did not want to move, whilst others wanted to separate and go their own ways. All in all Abraham was having a hard time of it.

He blamed Eb Bream. If Bream had not sought sanctuary in these hills that goddamn hunting party would not have shown up and they would not be in this mess. And there had been no sighting of Bream in the vicinity of the camp, which signified that Bream, having evaded discovery, had turned and headed back the way he had come. As Bream was running for his life it was unlikely he would show himself hereabouts but if he did, well, Abraham would not keep him around. Goddamn, Eb Bream, the cause of this catastrophe, would go into the cooking-pot forthwith; better he become hog-food sooner rather than later.

Moreover, Glenda Crocket had always been a respectable woman, but the same could not be said for Clara Bream, who had actually proposed to Kingdom Bream herself.

According to Glenda, Kingdom had stated that he would accept the proposal if Clara would walk through town naked. Clara had agreed, only stipulating that she would start walking just as dawn was breaking and that she would carry two Peacemakers and blast anyone she encountered during her walk. And she had done it too. But no one had been killed for not one eye had been about to see her. Clearly Eb Bream came from a family that was crazed. Too bad no one had known it or they would have let him be.

Eb Bream was worried about Samuel Pilgrim. The man lacked patience. And all Pilgrim wanted was his sister and her young ones; the rest of those taken captive by the Crockets could go to hell along with the Crockets as far as Pilgrim was concerned. That was not the right attitude.

Musgrave was riding with them. Not up into hill country, but Musgrave had volunteered to set up a base camp to receive those rescued by the other two. And Joe had gone so far as to draw a map showing the best trails to take.

'I am leaving you in charge, Joe,' Musgrave had said. 'Miz Jenny, she don't know nothing about running a ranch and nor does Miz Bliss, so I reckon it's up to you until I get back.' Joe had not replied but Musgrave had not been expecting a reply, Joe being such an awkward old cuss.

Samuel Pilgrim thinned his lips. He was mighty tired of hearing Eb tell him what had to be done, although he was obliged to admit that the plan Eb had come up with was amazingly simple and minimized the risk to themselves. He was obliged to listen now as Eb droned on about the necessity of tidying up. Musgrave, he noticed, had not mentioned the matter of the hunting party. He knew why. Musgrave would be hoping they were all dead. That way they were less of a problem. Kentish had after all, been Musgrave's boss for a mighty long time.

Peters knew he must have Miz Maud's ranch. There was a water-hole on her property that so far had never run dry. He needed her land. His herd was growing. He aimed to become one of the biggest suppliers of beef in the territory. He aimed to start a family and for that he needed a respectable woman used to the hardships of ranching life. Maud would do. Her late pa had been a tough old bastard, so the pedigree was good. And pedigree was important, he reflected, as he approached her ranch.

Ned, who was cleaning out the stable, saw him coming and ran towards the ranch house. Peters thinned his lips. First off he would order Ned to collect his gear and head for town. If Ned refused to oblige then he would of necessity have to blast the idiot.

Rosie Hobbs knew something was wrong. Ned was practically skipping as he spilled the beans.

'Just stay put, Ned. Sit down at the kitchen table and don't you move until I give the order,' she snapped.

Ned sat.

Rosie forgot about Ned. It was gonna be now, she reflected, sooner rather than later. She had no interest in how Peters had escaped his captors, no interest in what had become of the rest of that goddamn hunting party; she was focused solely on herself and how this man's arrival would relate to her existence.

She was tired of moving around and hiring out her gun to the highest bidder. She liked it here, working for Miz Maud. And when Howie proposed she aimed to accept. She'd keep working here and he could keep his livery barn going and, well, they'd work things out.

Floyd dismounted. 'Hello the house. You come on out, Miz Maud.' She lacked the guts to try and blast him, he reflected. Nevertheless he was alert for movement at the window.

The front door opened and a woman came out on to the porch.

'I'm Hobbs,' she declared. 'Ramrod of this ranch. State your piece.'

'Hobbs!' He'd heard of her. He hesitated momentarily. He'd heard talk of how she had been lucky, how she was not top-notch and how most of the tales

145

about her were pure fiction. Her reputation, men had said, had been built on lies. Well, that figured. She was here working for Maud because no one else would hire her. And Maud knew that there was no way anyone else would hire out to ramrod a ranch wanted by Floyd Peters.

'You ain't needed,' he stated flatly. 'I'll bring in my own ramrod.' He hesitated to insult her although he felt like doing so. 'Me and Miz Maud are engaged. We'll be tying the knot mighty soon. I don't want you around so I am telling you to leave. And take those two critters that call themselves ranch hands with you.'

'I ain't leaving. Back away, Peters. You've been lucky, so it seems, but your luck ain't going to last if you tangle with me. And you are a damn liar. Miz Maud cannot stand the sight of you!'

A string of profanities left his lips. Even as he spoke he reached for his Peacemaker.

She had known he was going to do it. His kind was totally predicable. His chauvinism would not let him believe that she could best him. She felt herself to be invincible. She knew she was faster. Her faith in herself was unshakeable. It was with disbelief that she registered agonizing pain as she began to fall.

Floyd Peters stood over the downed woman. She was not dead. 'Looks like you've met your match, Hobbs.' He pointed his gun at her forehead. 'You're nothing but a mangy old dog and I am gonna put you out of your misery.' He felt the trigger beneath his finger and began to ease back, prolonging the moment for the fullest enjoyment.

He never saw the man who took aim at his broad back. The old buffalo gun almost blasted him into two halves. His own shooter discharged into the air as he fell.

Juan dropped the smoking rifle and hobbled towards Miz Rosie, yelling out for Ned to get himself out and lend a hand. As for Peters, he could just stay where he fell; there weren't no one around here gonna break their back digging him a grave. Although, knowing Miz Maud, she would likely insist upon the body being toted into town. As for Miz Rosie, he surely hoped she pulled through. He had seen wounds before and she looked as though she would.

'Why, thank you, Juan,' Rosie muttered.

'No need to thank me, Miz Rosie. It was a pleasure,' he replied. 'Now you're gonna make it or I'll have Howie after me!'

Abraham Crocket reckoned he was facing a mutiny and the leader was his nephew Walt, son of Bertram, Abraham's elder brother.

'I reckon I'm shipping out.' Walt stood firm. 'I'm damn tired of hiding out for something I never done. And there ain't nobody cares nowadays what Grandma did way back. There ain't nobody looking for me. I aim to change my name. I'm gonna call myself Mr Brown.'

'You ain't going,' Abraham snarled. 'How long do you think you're gonna last out there. You ain't capable of taking care of yourself. There ain't nothing going to change. We're gonna carry on just like

Ma were here. That way we stay alive.'

'The hell you say!'

'The hell I do!'

'Make me.' Walt threw down the challenge.

'I'm gonna stomp the stuffing out of you,' Abraham moved forward, stopping abruptly as Walt pulled a blade.

'That ain't gonna stop me!' he snarled.

The two men circled each other warily whilst the rest of the clan formed a circle around them. Abraham began to recognize that only one of them could walk away from this alive. He kicked out, hoping to kick the knife out of Walt's hand but Walt danced away, changing his knife from hand to hand as he probed for an advantage. To get out of this damn prison he must of necessity kill his uncle and in the ugliest fashion possible to discourage anyone else from butting in and telling him he had got to stay.

In the prison hut they heard the commotion and knew that the Crockets had turned upon each other. Not that it mattered in the least. They were all done for and they knew it.

Walt lunged and he was pretty damn quick but Uncle Abe was quicker. Abraham dodged back, wondering if he was gonna be lucky again the next time the little varmint tried to stick him. The problem was, Walt's stamina would last out longer. Why the hell didn't one of the clan fell Walt from behind! There they all stood like so many dummies without the wits to intervene. The outcome of this was gonna affect the whole damn bunch of them.

From his vantage point in the trees Bream, raising a spyglass to his eye, studied the watch-tower. It was empty. And from the shouts coming from the far side of the stockade it seemed the whole damn bunch was otherwise engaged. Crouching low, he approached warily, knowing damn well what to expect if those varmints got their hands on him.

Walt saw Abraham was flagging. And prepared to launch his attack, but before he could make his move their world disintegrated around them as the watch-tower went flying high. The sound of the explosion caused those who did not fall to the ground to scatter as pieces of broken wood showered down upon them. Without a doubt they were under attack and those who could think expected the attackers to come charging in, guns blazing.

CHAPTER ELEVEN

As the fence was blasted sky high Bream hoped Pilgrim's kin were safe. If they had been harmed Pilgrim would be sure to hold him personally responsible.

Kids and women were screaming and crying. Some were bloodied. All were in shock. Abraham Crocket was the first to find his wits. He took charge. He had to. Taking charge of the clan was his burden now his ma was gone.

'We'll settle our differences later,' he croaked. 'We've got more important matters to deal with. Eb Bream has made his move against us. Get the men together. We'll unleash the dogs. We might be able to get to him before they tear him to pieces.'

'It's Peters. The Lord be praised,' a waddy croaked. 'He's back to save us.'

'Maybe,' another rejoined. But he was beginning to have doubts concerning Floyd Peters.

Kentish fixed bloodshot eyes on the two youngsters, who had come running into the prison hut, young boys not yet of an age and hopefully not too bright! They'd been given a chance, a chance to escape!

'In my pocket,' he croaked, 'I've got a mighty fine watch. It's yours for a drink of cool water.'

The younger of the two approached. Clearly the miserable little varmint wanted that pocket-watch.

'Jeremiah!' he heard the woman scream. The boy hesitated. Kentish guessed the screamer was the varmint's ma.

'Take the watch,' Tony urged. 'Hell, boy, I ain't going to need it and my own boy, well, he ain't with me.'

Jeremiah, still hesitating, was close enough now. Staking everything Tony grabbed him and held him fast. As expected the other little varmint ran off, yelling for his ma.

'What the hell are you doing?' Robinson mumbled.

'Bargaining. Just bargaining,' Kentish grunted.

A woman burst into the shed, rifle in her hand.

'Don't you think it,' Kentish bellowed. 'Because before you can blast me I'm gonna snap his neck unless get me the keys! You lot are done for! Your men ain't coming back. Now if you want this boy to live you fetch me that goddamn key!'

'Do it, Ma. Give him the key,' the boy yelled.

The woman fled. Kentish kept hold of the squirming little varmint. His only hope was that these women were so used to being told what to do that none of them knew how to think for herself. It was a long shot but it was all he had. He wasn't waiting

151

here to be slaughtered. From outside he could hear shrieking as the women argued.

Eden Crocket, sitting at his kitchen table holding a blood-soaked rag to his temple, refused to hand over the keys. His ankle was broke, he thought, and he was in no mood to listen to the woman's gabbling.

'You damn fool. The man is bluffing. He ain't gonna wring Jeremiah's neck. He'll be able to guess what the boys would do to him when they get back. Besides which, Jeremiah ain't no great loss. He's sickly, too sickly to grow into a fine Crocket. You'll lose him anyway. Now get out of my sight! Go tend them that needs it.'

'I will, Eden, I will,' she bleated. Behind Eden a careworn toothless woman picked up a stone jug and with a scream brought it down hard on his head. She whacked him again for good measure. Eden collapsed over the table, if not dead now, well on the way to it. Jeremiah's ma grabbed up the keys and ran to save her son.

'Come on, woman, come on,' Kentish yelled, mad with terror that something could go wrong. 'Set me free!' He kept hold of Jeremiah just in case.

'Give it here,' a waddy raged, grabbing the key from the woman. Just then there was one hell of another explosion, nearby but not in the camp itself.

Kentish staggered out into the daylight. Chaos greeted him. Terrified women and children were running about like so many headless chickens. Kentish headed for the woods and comparative safety. He guessed the Crocket men had been led into a trap.

*

They were following him now, the whole darn bunch of them, intent upon retribution. Bream glanced over his shoulder, trying to judge the distance between himself and the pursuers. He did not doubt that Pilgrim would keep his nerve nor that Pilgrim would have any qualms about blowing him sky high with the rest of them. Not for the first time Eb wished he had never picked up that goddamn doll. But it was too late for maybes now. He rode for his life.

Samuel Pilgrim wiped a trickle of sweat from his brow. The time had got to be right. He was impressed by the way Bream had set the explosives. It seemed Bream had been a railroad man before he had settled down and become a respectable telegraph clerk purely to please his wife.

Pilgrim shifted his position slightly. He lay belly down amongst the scrub, waiting for Bream. Nearby there was movement and a rattler slithered into view. Pilgrim did not so much as twitch and the snake moved on its way.

And then he heard the sound of a rider and Bream rode by, of necessity moving slowly for one did not ride hell for leather through this scrub. Pilgrim could hear the dogs now as they gave pursuit.

Pilgrim felt amazingly calm. He waited until the Crockets, riding bunched together, were level. And then he pressed the plunger and brought hell to the world. When he was able Pilgrim rose to his feet. He ignored the carnage. His stomach did not churn as he walked through it. His only thought was to find his sister and his nieces. Bream could do the clearing up. Any suffering critter had to be put out of its misery and that included the Crockets. It was almost over. They'd done it. They had wiped out this bunch of murdering varmints.

Kentish staggered into the woods and crawled beneath a low, spiked, overhanging bush. Near by, Robinson had thrown himself upon one of the fleeing women as he screeched obscenities at her. But he was not to have his pleasure for another woman appeared; screeching hysterically, she plunged a knife into Robinson's back and then both women fled.

On his belly, Robinson tried for one desperate moment to scrabble forward before he collapsed dead.

'Damn fool,' Kentish muttered. 'Damn fool.'

Someone was coming now, whistling cheerfully. Kentish tensed; if that man were Eb Bream Lord help him he'd be upon him and kill him with his bare teeth if needs be. But the man was not Bream. He was shorter, stouter, with hair worn in a long braid that reminded Kentish of Indian Joe. Why, the two-timing old varmint had contrived their downfall, deliberately leading them up a trail which he knew would be the death of them, deliberately letting them ride into Crocket territory knowing damn well what their fate would be.

'I will have retribution,' Kentish muttered. The varmints would pay. All of them! Bream, Floyd, and old Joe.

*

'Mister . . .' An escaped waddy staggered towards Samuel Pilgrim, convinced that Pilgrim was his saviour. Pilgrim shot him out of hand. The varmint had been after Bream, after all, and as such Pilgrim considered he posed a threat.

'I ain't here to kill folk,' Pilgrim yelled, the irony of his words lost upon him. 'Them womenfolk who were held here by force, well, I've come to get you out of it. There are wagons and victuals waiting back there to get you back to town. Just get yourselves where I can see you.'

Someone had let the hogs out and they were fleeing now, heading into the woods. He saved his bullets. There were worse than the hogs that might have to be dealt with.

A woman appeared and then another, cowed-looking creatures towing scrawny youngsters and there, running towards him, came the girls but there was no sign of their ma. His heart fell. Before he left this hell-hole he was going to burn it to the ground. There was going to be no shelter nor any victuals for anyone who might have fled to come back to.

'Come on!' He was suddenly weary of the whole damn business. 'We're heading out. We're all going home.' From afar he heard the sound of gunfire and guessed that Bream was tidying up, dispatching any luckless critter that had not been killed outright. Well, it had to be done, he reflected.

Tony Kentish planned his survival. He must find and

kill one of the hogs. The fool woman had left her knife sticking out of Robinson, which Kentish had been quick to retrieve. And he must follow the river; that way he would not die of thirst. It would take him longer, but leastways he would get home. He had three of them to deal with now; Bream, Peters and old Joe. After that he did not much care what happened. With Travis gone he felt his life was all but over. He was suffering and he was going to make goddamn sure the other three went out suffering.

Eb Bream could not believe it was over. It had been hell. He and Pilgrim had got the women and kids, some of whom seemed deranged, back to the waiting wagons. Musgrave had taken charge then, leaving Pilgrim to care for his two nieces and Bream to reflect whether he ought to head back up into the hills and search for Kentish. But his heart was not in it. All he wanted was to get back to Miz Jenny. And if Kentish had survived, sooner or later he would show up!

Tony Kentish walked into his empty ranch house. That goddamn bitch Juanita clearly expected that he had not made it. She was gone with all the fine clothes and jewellery that had belonged to Mrs Kentish and the loose cash that had been lying about. And some of the men, those who had not ridden with the hunting party, had quit, leaving a handful remaining who had professed cheer that he was back, not because they were glad of it but simply because they wanted to keep their jobs. As far as he knew he was the only one of the hunting party to have made it back safely, apart from Floyd who they had told him had been planted, blasted by Hobbs word was, who had been shot herself but was making a good recovery. And Bream was holed up at what had been the Bliss place, friends with Musgrave by all accounts.

Kentish bided his time. He waited until Sunday morning to make his move. Joe was going to be the first. He was going to skin the old buzzard and leave him for Bream to find. He'd see to Joe whilst the rest of them were at church. Musgrave was clearly demented for he'd taken to preaching on Sunday morning.

Joe settled down on the porch and began to think about the old days. He thought of them more and more, a sure sign that he was destined to quit this world in the near future. But not quite yet. Last night he had dreamed of his enemy. And now he waited, pretty damn certain that the man would come. In his dream he had seen how it would be.

There he was, the old bastard, sitting in the rocker, wrapped in a blanket. Kentish felt only triumph, clean forgetting about the man whose throat Joe had slit.

Kentish dismounted. The old fellow made no move to get out of the chair.

'This ain't going to be quick,' Kentish warned. 'I've been through hell on account of you and Bream. Leastways Bream did not know what was up there. But you did, you old devil. You're gonna pay.'

Bessie Bliss came round the side of the house. Her situation had improved somewhat and she was walking now, and even helping out some as poor old Joe was clearly going downhill. This was unavoidable considering his advanced years. In one large hand she carried a dead chicken, killed by herself, a considerable achievement given what Willard had done to her.

She heard every word spoken by Tony Kentish. She dropped the chicken and her hand closed over the stone in her pocket. Bessie had been raised on a farm. Early on she'd found ways of dispatching chickens which did not necessitate running after them. Without thought she hurled the missile. Kentish went down as though he had been poleaxed.

Joe's strength returned. He moved quickly, binding Kentish's wrists and ankles and gagging him as well before he turned his attention to Miz Bessie, who had collapsed on the ground and was having one of her turns.

'Now don't you worry,' he advised. 'I'll cook the chicken soup. You just get yourself to bed and I'll bring your tea. You need to sleep, Miz Bessie.' He'd be sure to make a brew that would put Bessie to sleep for an hour or so. That would give him enough time to deal with Kentish.

When Kentish came round he found himself face downward over a horse, bound and gagged and helpless.

'Eb Bream, Sam Pilgrim, Miz Rosie,' Joe said quite loudly, 'Let me tell you, boss Kentish, when I was a young man I was more dangerous than those three

158

put together. I never thought I would see the day when I would work for a dog like boss Peters. I'm gonna end my days snoozing in Miz Bessie's old rocker and that's a fact. And as for you, Miz Bessie killed you and I planted you deep. And that's what I'm gonna do. Ain't no one gonna want to know where you've been planted, ain't no one gonna want to dig you up and take a look. You're done for. You should have shown some respect and before you die you're gonna know it.'

At that moment Kentish would have been glad to have seen Eb Bream. At least Bream would have made it quick.

'Why, if Eb Bream were to show up and want to dispatch you quick I would kill him myself,' Joe continued. 'For I ain't a merciful man, boss Kentish. And you chose to make me your enemy. Nor am I a fool. If I let you live you would come back determined upon the retribution you see as your right. And it is my right to do to you what you were going to do to me.'

Eb Bream closed his eyes as Musgrave droned on. Miz Jenny sure as hell was a contrary woman.

'Why, Eb, you know the respectable folk of this town don't like the idea of me sitting in church alongside them. And that's precisely why I aim to do it. There ain't no harm in us reminding the respectable folk of this town that they were more than willing to countenance a great wrong.'

Eb snoozed. There was no help for it, he could not get away. And he kind of suspected Miz Jenny was enjoying playing at being respectable. He would never dare say so. Pilgrim, across the aisle along with his nieces, was wide awake, Eb had noted. He guessed it was safe to snooze. If Tony Kentish were to come bursting in Sam Pilgrim would take care of him, that was for sure. And then, for the oddest moment, Eb felt a presence as though the ghost of Kentish, a man whom he had only seen from afar and never even exchanged the time of day with, were at his shoulder. He sat up with a start. Gave a shake of his head, admonishing himself for his foolishness and went back to sleep, mindful that Miz Jenny's elbow would wake him when Musgrave was done.